Soaring Passion
In Eagle Hills

KRISTINE CABOT

Jan-Carol
Publishing, Inc
"every story needs a book"

Soaring Passion in Eagle Hills
Kristine Cabot

Published November 2018
Fiery Night
Imprint of Jan-Carol Publishing, Inc.
All rights reserved
Copyright © 2018 by Kristine Cabot

ISBN: 978-1-945619-78-6
Library of Congress Control Number: 2018961924

You may contact the publisher:
Jan-Carol Publishing, Inc.
PO Box 701
Johnson City, TN 37605
publisher@jancarolpublishing.com
jancarolpublishing.com

This book is dedicated to those who refuse to accept the concept that maturity means the end of deep rousing sensuality and warm romantic love.

Dear Reader

Step into the small coastal town of Eagle Hills, North Carolina, where Lily and Max experience a circle of secrets, murder under a political arena, and the magic of unbridled lust. This fictitious story brings a hint of reality, a touch of mystery, and a fulfillment of hidden desires. Follow this couple on their personal journey as they discover each other and the joys of mature passion.

Acknowledgments

I wish to acknowledge my public relations agent, my personal assistant, my dedicated publisher, and those who have supported and encouraged me to make this book a reality.

Chapter 1

When Lily Roberts took the job at Cumberland Enterprise thirty-four years ago, her plan was to stay until she found a better opportunity. Being an executive secretary for one of the larger companies in the area had its perks. She soon realized that jobs like hers were few in the small town of Hoggville, nestled in the Appalachian Mountains of Tennessee. So, she settled in for the long haul. The company found her eager to learn, as well as smart in both daily operations and people skills. As a well-respected employee, her job became her career—and eventually, her second home. But after her husband of many years, Joe, passed away suddenly, Lily's reputation became "poor pitiful Lil." Hardly a week went by that someone didn't question why Joe was found dead in a motel room by the local sheriff.

Life with Joe had been a journey with a man she had known forever. There had been ups and downs. He never got physically abusive, but his words echoed long after he apologized. Early in the marriage, Lily's mother gave her only one piece of advice, "You made your bed, now lie in it." Divorce was never an option, not in a town where gossip ran rampant and sides were taken more often than not under half-truths. Lily had been thrown onto a different path. She retired from a job that gave her sanctuary for many years. Now, she answered to no one.

Always seeking ways to save a dollar and pinch a penny, through the years, Lily accumulated a substantial nest egg with the hopes of seeing the world outside of the mountains. With a handful of travel brochures from a local AAA, she spent hours reading, gazing at the photos, and imagining herself sipping a glass of wine on the coast of Italy. Joe never seemed interested in travel. Since he passed, she felt like she was creating an adventure of her own. The farthest Lily traveled out of town was a honeymoon trip to Dollywood for a weekend.

Late one night, as she watched a Hallmark movie in bed, the phone rang. To her surprise, it was her cousin Annie, from North Carolina. The last time they spoke, it was the day of Joe's funeral. Annie had apologized for being unable to attend the service and promised to keep in touch.

"Annie, it is so good to hear from you. How are you doing?" Lily asked.

"Lily, that's why I'm calling. I wanted to check on you, and see if perhaps you could come to Eagle Hills for a few days," Annie said.

"Now that my time is my own, I would love to come to visit."

"Since it's just the two of us left, I have some important mementos for you. Being the oldest cousin, I seem to have inherited the family photos and keepsakes," Annie said. "I want you to have them all."

"Why do you want to part with our family history?"

"Honey, my health is failing...and I need to discuss some things with you. After all, I am ten years older."

"I know you were too sick to travel for Joe's funeral. Are you any better?"

"I still can't travel, but I need to see you," Annie said.

Even though her cousin's voice was even and calm, Lily knew this was an important request. "Of course; I will come right away. I'll leave tomorrow."

"Thank you, Honey. Please plan to stay a few days."

Although it meant driving alone to North Carolina, Lily packed her bag the next day. She asked a neighbor to keep an eye on her house while she was gone. Then, she headed east, toward the coastal town of Eagle Hills. She didn't have any definite plans. Lily didn't know how long she'd stay but Annie needed her, and that's all that mattered.

When Lily arrived at her cousin's beach cottage, she was met at the door by a hospice nurse. The nurse introduced herself and quickly brought Lily up to speed on Annie's medical condition. Sadly, Lily's visit with her cousin lasted only ten days. Lily held her hand, told her she loved her when her cousin took her last breath. According to Annie's wishes, there was no funeral service. In the will, the beachfront cottage and all her belongings were left to Lily. Instead of returning home to Tennessee after the burial, she stayed several days longer. There at the cottage, with the sounds of the ocean, she found peace. She walked the beach. She mourned her cousin, her parents, and her husband. Lily quietly fell in love with the little town of Eagle Hills, the pristine beach, and the large sprawling oak trees.

Reluctantly, she returned to her hometown. Being alone in the old house filled with decades of memories quickly fostered a gnawing feeling of emptiness. She knew she needed to make a change. Reaching outside her comfort zone was huge leap of faith she was willing to take. Lily called a realtor and put her house up for sale. It didn't last a week on the buyers' list; the town gossip and unfounded speculations basically sold the house for her. Friends and neighbors were miffed that she was leaving the mountains, almost demanding an explanation. She gave none—with the exception of her best friend, Joanie.

Lily sold nearly everything she could not pack in five cardboard boxes, which she prepared and mailed to her new home. After cramming her SUV with clothes and some family heirlooms, she left the Tennessee mountains and its people for a new start in North Carolina. Joanie pleaded with her to not make such a rash decision, leaving her hometown where she had spent all her life. Rarely did anyone leave Hoggville, Tennessee for good. Sometimes, a young adult would take off for parts unknown, but eventually, they would return to the security of the mountains. At one point, Lily asked Joanie to pack up and come along.

Joanie flirted with the notion for a while. "Maybe I'll come and visit, once you're settled."

"I would really love that. You know you're welcome anytime," Lily said.

Choosing the little town of Eagle Hills to make her new life wasn't as difficult for Lily as she anticipated. She was intrigued by the crashing waves. The sun rising over the beauty of the sea brought a serenity she desperately sought. Never having touched an ocean before the visit to her cousin, she marveled at the frothy salt water tickling her feet. She felt childlike when squishing the sand between her toes.

Once she settled into the little cottage, Lily realized that the rooms were sparsely furnished. She spent much of her time shopping in the quaint antique stores. With the cool breezes of autumn approaching, the sounds of the sea birds and ocean waves felt even more invigorating during her long walks on the beach. She didn't mind living alone; being alone was soothing. There was no rush to create a social life. She wasn't looking for male companionship, and sex didn't cross her mind. Had she stayed in Tennessee, her only identity would have been an old barren widow woman. In Eagle Hills, she refused to accept that label. She had failed Joe miserably, as he often reminded her. She vowed to never again allow a man into her life.

In Eagle Hills, Lily quickly fell into a personal routine of enjoying simple things that her life with Joe never offered. Whether watching a sunrise, foaming waves, or rolling dark clouds full of lightning and distant thunder, she felt a closeness, a comfort with nature. Of course, she missed her mountains: the changing of the seasons in the holler, the fresh mountain air. She would always be a Tennessee girl. Long telephone chats with Joanie kept that connection.

Early one morning, after her daily walk on the beach, Lily poured a cup of coffee and called her best friend. "Hey, Joanie. What are you up to?"

"Oh, Lily! It's so good to hear from you. Are you settled in?" Joanie asked. "I've been thinking about you."

"Getting more settled every day. I wish you were here. I was just getting a little homesick, so I thought I would call."

"I hope it's me you're missing, and not that son of a bitch you buried," Joanie said.

"What?"

"It was hard for me to watch him mistreat you all those years. He was never there for you, even when you miscarried those babies. I know that hurt."

"But you were there for me. I have always been able to count on you. Joe wanted children because he had no other family," Lily said.

"He sure consoled himself really well with all those whores—until the last one gave him a heart attack."

"I couldn't be the woman he needed, Joanie."

"You are a better woman than he ever deserved, and you're the best friend I could ever hope for. When are you coming to see me?" Lily asked.

"I promise to come soon," Joanie replied.

Chapter 2

Life on the beach gave her a kind of acceptance that allowed her to be herself. On a cool afternoon in September, she sat on the worn, wooden bench right outside her cottage door, simply enjoying her freedom. With a quilt wrapped around her shoulders, consumed by her thoughts, she was oblivious to the large animal loping down the path to the beach area. For whatever reason, known only to the dog kingdom, a golden Labrador Retriever snatched the edge of Lily's quilt, dragging it down toward the ocean's edge.

Lily jumped up and chased after the dog. "Hey, dog! Come back here!" She caught up with the animal and grabbed the quilt in a tug of war. "Let go!"

A strong commanding voice came from behind Lily. "Sam! Stop! Come here now!"

The dog immediately released the quilt and ran to her master. Lily turned around to see a man dressed in tan cargo shorts, his khaki shirt unbuttoned. A fedora like the one worn by Indiana Jones completed his masculine look. He held the dog's leash in one hand.

"I apologize for Sam's behavior. She knows better," he said. "She's a service dog, retired now. I think she likes being retired more than I do." He laughed.

Lily stumbled as she took a step in the soft sand. The man reached for her hand, breaking her fall. Now she felt embarrassed. "Thanks. I just didn't want to lose this old quilt. It's a family thing," she said. "No harm done."

Gently squeezing her hand, the man smiled. "By the way, my name is Max. My companion here is Samantha, but answers to Sam. And yours?"

Lily found herself drawn to his tanned, bare chest. But it was his eyes that were hypnotizing her, that stirred her inner feelings. "Lily," she answered. She tried hard to think of something more to say but failed. She smiled, feeling so awkward.

"Good to meet you, Lily," Max said. For those moments, neither was aware they were still holding hands until he reached to put the leash on Sam. He grinned as he let go of Lily's hand. "Have a good evening."

"You too," she said. She felt flushed, in a shy young girl sort of way. She started walking back to her bench. *I can't believe this. I couldn't open my mouth! I just stood there like a dummy. His eyes... Oh, my. Now wait a minute, I'm an old woman. What is wrong with me? Whew!* Lily stopped midway back to the bench and turned to see Max still standing there, watching her. They waved. Then she watched this man named Max run down the beach with his dog. *Oh my, he looks good,* she thought. *I'll bet he thinks I'm some crazy woman. Why in the world did I do that? I wish Joanie was here. She's been single for a long time, like forever. Well, not counting that marriage to that dumbass who nearly beat her to death.*

Lily muffled a laugh as she went inside her cottage. She grabbed her cell phone out of an old ceramic ashtray to call Joanie, but quickly changed her mind. Instead, she slipped the phone in her pocket and went back out the door.

The destination was her favorite store, just a few blocks away. She enjoyed the walk, using the time to collect her thoughts and reflect on her chance meeting with a stranger who gave her goosebumps. As Lily opened the door to Books4U, she was greeted by the owner and new friend, Debra, a vivacious woman who possessed a wealth of knowledge through books and personal experience. Debra had grown up on a farm in southern Ohio. Unable to attend college, she was self-taught in many subjects. Early on, she owned a clothing store in Fairfield for decades. Lily and Debra became fast friends during her initial stay in Eagle Hills. They had much in common: both from small towns, both widowed, and both enjoyed losing themselves in the pages of a good book.

"Lily, I'm going to be closing up in a few minutes. Do you want to go across the street and have a drink?" Debra asked.

"Sure. That's exactly what I need," Lily said.

Debra grabbed the keys while Lily hung the *Closed* sign on the door. Across the street was Ernie's Nest, a favorite bar of the locals. Visitors were always welcome but usually found it quite boring, compared to the exciting nightlife a few miles down the road.

Lily and Debra didn't have to order their drinks. When they entered the dimly-lit room, the bartender, Ernie, poured their drinks and set the glasses on the bar. He had flirted with Lily ever since she'd moved to Eagle Hills, but she made it very clear that she didn't want a man in her life. She'd told Ernie up front that she wouldn't have another man, even if he was handed to her on a silver platter.

"Thank you, Ernie." Debra said. "Today has been...long. And tedious."

He smiled. "I know what you mean. Business has been slow this week."

"Ernie, do you have any chips?" Lily asked. "I hate to drink on an empty stomach. It makes me a little goofy."

They laughed. Ernie set a small dish of chips down in front of Lily. His hand brushed against hers as she reached for a chip.

"Excuse me, Ernie," Lily said.

"No problem," Ernie said, thinking *I wish she could see me as more than just a friend.*

"OK, Lily, what is going on in that mind of yours?" Debra asked. "And don't say nothing because I know better than that. Spill it, girlfriend."

Lily started to tell her about the afternoon encounter when the door opened. The mystery man and his dog came in. Max slid into a booth, and Sam curled up next to him at his feet. The barmaid was a bit skittish about Sam, but Max explained she was a retired service dog. When Max was served his drink, the barmaid set a bowl of water down for Sam.

"Oh, crap," Lily whispered. She bowed her head, trying to hide her face.

"What in the hell are you doing?" Debra asked. "What's wrong with you?"

"You see that man over there with the dog? Well, I met him this afternoon on the beach. He's really very... Uh... Well, nice," Lily answered.

"OK, so why are trying to hide from him?" Debra asked. "You're acting silly. Turn around, get his attention, and say 'Hi' to him. You are allowed to do that, you know."

Lily took a huge gulp of her rum and Diet Coke, nearly choking, and turned just as he looked in her direction. He grinned. She nodded. Then, she leaned over to Debra.

"What did I just do? I made an idiot out of myself," Lily whispered. "Debra, don't you say a word."

Debra looked at Lily and rolled her eyes. "Go on over there and talk to him. Do it, or I'll embarrass the both of us. You're not in high school."

"No! Don't you dare. OK, I'm going. No, I can't. OK, give me a minute. You stay right here. I'm afraid of what you might say," Lily said.

Lily slid off the bar stool and walked over to Max. "Nice to see you again."

"Have a seat," Max said. "I swear I'm not a stalker." He chuckled.

A few minutes of friendly chat turned to thirty minutes before Lily realized she had abandoned Debra at the bar. But when she looked, the bartender shook his head to say she had already left.

"Oh my, I didn't mean to leave my friend alone. I sure did monopolize your time. Sorry about that. I guess I'd better get on home now," Lily said. She stood up to leave.

"It's time we head home too. Mind if we walk with you?"

Lily stuttered, "N-n-not at all. I welcome the company."

Max paid for his drink and left the barmaid a hefty tip. The walk was brief. Lily felt comfortable talking to him about living all her life in the mountains. She briefly mentioned her late husband, but gave no details other than he had died unexpectedly. She didn't realize until later that she still knew very little about Max. He controlled their conversation by letting her reminisce. Max was an expert in avoiding any conversations leading to his past or his present. It was a matter of his own survival, as well as a method of protecting those close to him.

When they reached her door, she didn't know whether to shake his hand or just thank him. He saw that she was nervous. He leaned over, cupped her face, and gently kissed her forehead. She trembled. This tender gesture brought an unfamiliar warmth to her body. She looked up at him. *Oh God,* she thought. *I can't breathe.*

He stepped back, looking into her eyes. Without another word, he turned and left. He couldn't breathe, either.

Chapter 3

A morning downpour beat against Lily's bedroom window, waking her from a deep sleep. For years, insomnia had ruled her nights. But since she'd moved, leaving her past behind, her sleep problems had eased somewhat. She continued to struggle in controlling her journey, yet she embraced the decisions she made. She grasped every opportunity to improve her body and mind. Sometimes, she felt selfish and unsure. It was a newfound world for her; it was *Lily's* world.

After the rain passed, Lily left for her morning walk along the beach. The air was invigorating, and the ocean sparkled in the dancing sunlight. The cool breeze caused her to zip up her jacket, reminding her that winter was near. She gathered a few shells along the water's edge, taking her time. It was a simple life, and she was content—or so she thought.

As Lily neared the edge of the pier, she saw several people watching a young boy lying in the sand. A man was on his knees, bent over the child and giving him CPR. A frantic woman stood over the child on the other side, hysterically flailing her arms. *This is going to end so badly*, Lily thought. Suddenly the boy gurgled, coughed, and opened his eyes. The paramedics arrived soon after and put him in the ambulance, along with the woman. Breathing hard, the hero stood up and rubbed his hands over his thick silver hair. The crowd cheered. Unaware that Lily was close behind him, Max turned around, nearly falling into her arms.

"Excuse me. I'm sorry," he said. "Lily, we meet again. Seems like we bump into each other a lot lately. Are you stalking me?"

"It seems so," she said. "Are you OK?" *Oh, his beautiful eyes.*

"Sure. A little out of breath, but nothing a good, cold drink couldn't fix."

"Where's Sam?"

"I left her at the cottage. I didn't plan on being gone but a minute or two. She's fine, though. She's watching television." He gave a faint laugh.

"I think I can help you. Sit down here on this plank. I'll run up on the pier and get you a drink. Don't leave."

Max nodded. "Don't worry. I'm not going anywhere."

Lily brought him a soda from the concession hut at the end of the pier. She figured it was too early for a beer.

After regaining his strength, Max offered to repay her. "Since we know each other so well, how about having a real drink with me this evening, around seven?"

Lily agreed before she even thought about it. She analyzed her answer, walking back to her cottage. *Yes, he seemed like a gentleman. He's pleasant enough. The dog likes him. He's easy on the eyes. Well, admit it Lily, he's got the sexiest eyes, the kind that look right through you. But hey, absolutely NOT! I'll never have another man in my bed again, much less in my life.* She burst out laughing, sure she looked like a crazy woman, mumbling and shaking her head.

Time dragged so slowly the rest of the day that Lily found herself changing clothes three times before deciding on a red top, black slacks, and red flats. Jewelry was minimal. *I don't want to look flashy.* She studied her body in the full-length mirror. She wasn't as perky as she had been ten years ago, yet she had always tried to keep herself from becoming a saggy old woman. Always blessed with a curvy body, she was still well endowed, which accentuated a tiny waist. She was proud of her hourglass figure. While she was married to Joe, he insisted on frumpy, oversized clothes and no makeup. Her hair had been a mousy brown, but thanks to Lady Clairol, she now wore a soft, auburn color on her shoulder-length bob.

Max knocked on her door ten minutes early. She was impressed. As they walked toward the local bar, he placed his hand at the base of her back, as if escorting her. Again, he took her breath away. *Stop it,* she thought. When they arrived at Ernie's Nest, they sat in a booth away from the chatter of patrons and the faint sound of music. Their conversation was easy: a few laughs, a couple of toasts for the young boy he saved, and then a quiet, easy feeling of comfort. Lily felt safe, and she liked it.

"You were amazing today," Lily said.

"Thank you," Max replied, obviously embarrassed. "I did what I thought would help. I couldn't just stand there. Believe me, I was worried the whole time."

She looked at him, *really* looked at him: his tanned face, his silver white hair, his captivating smile. But it was his eyes that she felt she could lose herself in—and probably every bit of her common sense, too.

As Vince Gill's latest love song played on the jukebox, Max stood up. "Dance with me?"

Lily didn't answer. She didn't have to, standing up before she formed the thought to do so. He led her to the small dance area and wrapped his arms around her. She wanted to break away, to run as fast as she could and never look back. Yet she clung to this new virgin desire, a deep longing her body had never felt. His firm hold guided her around the floor as if she was floating. No words needed. He felt his passion rising, something that hadn't happened in a very long time.

When the music stopped, Max gave her a friendly hug. "Thank you, Lily," he said. "I haven't danced in a while."

"You are very welcome. You're easy to follow," she said. "This has been such a nice evening. Thank you for inviting me out."

As they walked back to her cottage along the sandy path, he reached for her hand. Although surprised, she loved his simple touch. The night sky was filled with millions of stars. The moonlight seemed to follow them, opening up the darkness. At her door, she asked him if he wanted to come in for a cup of coffee. She didn't want the evening to end, and neither did he.

The coffee didn't get brewed. Once inside the cottage, he removed his shoes at the door. Lily started toward the kitchen. Unexpectedly, he slipped his arm around her waist and drew her close. She didn't resist. He kissed her soft waiting lips, and she responded. His hot breath on her neck brought chills as he gently kissed her nape. She gasped.

Max whispered, "Do you want me to leave?"

There was a moment of silence. "Don't leave," she said. Wrapped up in a whirlwind of desire, she wanted this man. It was complicated. She was afraid, but she wanted more. She couldn't explain it, but realized she just didn't care. His touch was controlling, yet, she felt empowered. She took him into her bedroom and stood in front of him, removing his white shirt. He felt helpless as he watched her undress him. Still fully clothed, she sat on the edge of the bed, unbuckled his belt, and slowly unzipped his pants. As his pants slid down his muscular legs, she admired his hard, mature body. She pulled him closer and kissed his stomach. He moaned, his body trembling.

Lily wasn't a stranger to sex after such a long marriage, but she had never been afforded the pleasure of enjoying it. Feeling as if there was a wildfire in her body, she did not hold back on her lust for the outline in his briefs. She removed his underwear, releasing his pulsating shaft, and for a moment, admired his strength.

Caught up in his rising desire to please this woman, he raised her arms above her head, took off her shirt, and released her bra. After laying her back on the bed, he removed her shoes and slacks. He gathered her legs, easing her to the middle of the bed. Slipping off her panties, he kissed her thighs, arousing intense animal urges. Lying beside her, he watched her breasts heaving in excitement. He drew her to him, his calloused hands softly touching her body, wanting to please her in every way. He moved down her body, exploring every inch with slow, feathered kisses. When he gently nibbled on her firm nipples, she moaned. She made him feel powerful. He ached to fulfill her most secret yearnings. He wanted all of her.

The silver fox felt her body rise as her moist desire craved his attention. He slipped his tongue into her wet mound and licked it. She grabbed his hair.

"Max, please...please," Lily cried out as she dug her fingers into his strong shoulders. Her urges had been locked up deep inside for so long.

Wildly aroused, he rose up and entered her, giving her everything that had been pent-up for months. As they released their passions, Lily rode the waves of ecstasy.

Exhausted and satisfied, he held her in his arms as they drifted off into a much-needed slumber. After midnight, Lily woke and reached for the man who had brought her such pleasure. His side of the bed was empty. The moonlight cast the shadow of Max, already dressed and standing by the window, across from the foot of the bed. She watched him without saying a word, as he seemed to be in deep thought. He turned to see her watching.

"You know I can't stay," he said.

Lily smiled. "I know," she replied, even though she didn't have a clue why he couldn't spend the night. She slipped her robe on and stood beside him. *Stay with me, please,* she thought.

"I'm scared. I've never been this confused. You know, I'm a Marine, but I have never felt so scared. Forgive me, I've got to leave."

Lily searched for the right words. "It's OK." She gently kissed his shoulder, not knowing what else to do.

Max held her close, brushing her tousled hair from her eyes. "You are so beautiful. I never expected any of this. Thank you."

"Neither did I. Thank you too," she answered.

He kissed her softly on the check before he left. It was a strange ending for a night of such raw passion. She wondered if she would ever see him again. She crawled back in bed and pulled the covers up over her head, as if to hide a myriad of feelings. She felt a bit guilty and a little embarrassed. *Am I too old to behave like this?* The night had brought forth a flood of emotions and confusion. She held the bed pillow close, savoring his scent. Soon, she fell asleep.

* * *

Out on the beach, Max faded into the dark. He walked so fast, he soon broke into a run. He needed to get back home. He needed a drink. He needed to stop thinking. He needed...

When he opened his door, he was greeted by his best friend. Sam immediately brought him the leash. "Sam, are you ready for a walk? I'm sorry I got tied up. I know it's late. Come on, girl, let's go," Max said, hooking the leash on her collar.

They walked at a faster pace than usual. Although wanting to hurry, he stopped just to appreciate the magnificent, star-filled sky connecting to the vast and uncontrollable ocean. Max had always been a planner, and now he felt unglued. Being alone on the beach or in life was never a concern for Max. He could take care of himself—and if necessary, Sam was trained to protect on command. By the time they returned home, Max was ready to call it a night. He took a shower, crawled into bed, and motioned for Sam to join him. The dog had slept on the foot of the bed ever since Max rescued her. The bond between this man and his dog was absolute. Max drifted off to sleep before he finished his prayers.

Chapter 4

A fresh cup of early morning coffee cleared her head. Lily found herself humming as she poured herself a second cup. She giggled. Her world was right and beautiful. Trying to subdue or reason away the excitement of the night before became impossible. She decided that even if she never saw him again, it was the most amazing night of her otherwise mundane existence. She would treasure it forever.

Lily filled the day with an unusual burst of energy. She chose not to waste it. Her morning was spent cleaning and doing laundry. After lunch, she kicked back in her recliner with a tall glass of iced tea. That was her reward. Even while watching her favorite soap opera, her mind wandered, reliving her night of passion. The characters on the long-running series could never compare to what she experienced with Max. She had been satisfied by a man with experience, a man who knew how to please. Life was good, for the moment.

Lily kept her cell phone on full charge. She carried it around with her from room to room all day, but no call came. Then, the doubts crept in. She wondered if she had done the wrong thing, going to bed with a man she hardly knew. Being born and raised in the hills and hollers deep in the Appalachian Mountains, she always abided by doing the proper thing. Finally, she decided to go see Debra. She needed someone to either calm her down and dispel her worries or tell her she did a stupid thing and to get over it. She wasn't ready for either.

Unfortunately, when Lily arrived at the bookstore, Debra was having an author event. The front area of the store was crowded with fans of Brock Savage, the New York best-selling author. He was conversing with the patrons standing in line holding his new novel, waiting for his signature. He looked just like the photo on the back of his books: tall, white hair pulled back in a long ponytail, chiseled features, and an inviting smile. He wore a navy T-shirt under a cream-colored sports jacket and looked quite fit in his tight jeans. Lily noticed he wore very little jewelry, just a small, gold, chain necklace and a functional watch, no rings.

On impulse, Lily picked up the new novel and eased her way into the line of excited customers. She had read his works in the past and actually thought he was very talented. But lately, she hadn't had the time, nor the inclination to read his edgy political mysteries. It seemed there was always a thread of truth woven in his stories, leaving the reader to wonder.

Brock Savage spent most of life in the military arena. However, his last position was a senior military advisor to the secretary of state, which earned him notoriety during a crisis that cost him his job. To the public, his retirement was a huge surprise. To those who were privy to foreign affairs, his so-called retirement was inevitable.

Lily placed the book in front of him. "I am quite a follower of yours."

Brock didn't bother to answer her. He scribbled his name inside the book. But as he handed the book back to her, he glanced up. "Thank you. And you are?"

"Lily."

"OK, Lily. I appreciate the compliment. Hope you enjoy my latest conspiracy mystery."

She smiled. "I'm sure I will."

Brock's face turned somber. "Stay safe."

She nodded. *That was weird,* she thought.

Lily found Debra in a throng of customers. She knew it was not a good time to chat. Slowly, she got to the counter. She saw how frazzled Debra looked, so she paid for the book and whispered, "I'll catch you later. We have *got* to talk."

Debra winked.

When Lily arrived home, she called Joanie back in Tennessee. She had to talk to someone. She really didn't want advice, she just needed a listener. The problem with Joanie was she was always full of advice, even though she never took any herself. Lily didn't hold back in telling her about Max.

"You did *what*?!" Joanie screeched through the phone. "Are you telling me the truth? You actually slept with a *stranger*?"

"Oh, Joanie, I don't need you to preach to me. I really got a good feeling from him. He seems to be a nice man."

"Well, he sure ain't a stranger to you now. I can't believe *you*, of all people, did that. Was he any good?"

"For heaven's sake, I didn't call you to brag. I just don't know what to do now. I don't even have his phone number! I don't know where he lives, either."

"Well then, there ain't much you can do but just back off and wait. If he *is* still interested in you, he'll contact you in one way or another. I'd go back to that bar. At least if he comes in, you're giving him a chance. You sure don't know much about a man who was bare-ass naked in your bed."

Lily laughed. She decided calling Joanie was not going to solve her problem. "That's a good idea, Joanie. I'll keep you informed. Call me in a few days. You know you can always come here for a visit. It's OK to get out of the holler for a change. I would love to see you."

"Well, I may have to come now and try to keep you on the straight and narrow. Or, if your feller has a friend, you can introduce me, and we can double date like we did in high school."

"Yeah, if things turn out good, I'll let you know," Lily said. "Oh, and by the way, he was perfect."

The call ended on a good note. Lily went to bed early that night, but sleep didn't come. She tossed and turned, finally getting back up and reading a few pages of the Savage novel, hoping it would put her to sleep. At 3 a.m., she closed her eyes.

A brilliant flash of lightning, followed by a loud crack of thunder jarred Lily to wake, with her heart racing. A late autumn rainstorm wasn't unusual in North Carolina, especially since it was hurricane season. She shuffled to the kitchen for her morning routine of coffee and an occasional honey bun. The caffeine charged her mind while the sugar boosted her energy. She admitted it wasn't healthy; she always had plans to change her diet, but they seemed to fade with the aroma of a warmed pastry.

Feeling a bit anxious, Lily decided to try to talk to Debra once again. Maybe they could grab a cup of coffee at Cheryl's Diner, the only diner within walking distance. Luckily, it was a slow day at the bookstore. Debra hung the *Closed* sign on the front door. At the diner, they grabbed an empty booth, and Cheryl came over to take their order.

Cheryl was a fixture in Eagle Hills. Her long, flashing red hair made her stand out among the regulars. Born and raised in Alabama, she came to Eagle Hills nearly forty years ago and bought the little diner. She added a couple of rooms in the back of the diner and called it home. Fiercely bold and brash, she had a heart of gold for those who struggled. On Sundays, she often prepared a meal for those less fortunate, at her own expense. No one talked about it; it was just something that she did.

"Hello, ladies. Do you need a menu, or have you already decided?" Cheryl asked. "Lily, I've not seen you a good while. Have you got a man keeping you hidden?"

Lily felt the heat of a blush. She looked at Debra. "Uh, no, I've just been busy."

Debra chimed in to break the awkward exchange. "Hey Cheryl, how about two coffees and a couple of pieces of your homemade pie?"

Cheryl smiled. "OK, be right back."

Debra and Lily made small talk until Cheryl had brought the coffee and pie. Debra was anxious to find out what was happening with the new man in Lily's life. "I'm dying to know. Are you still seeing that new feller? I'm sorry I couldn't talk to you the other day, but with all those customers, it just wasn't the right time. Oh, and I almost forgot to tell you that Brock Savage asked me about you. I mean, not that you would be interested—since you have a feller— but at least I let you know."

Lily shook her head. "Debra, I don't about you but I think that Brock Savage is kind of creepy. I have no specific reason; I just got a weird feeling from him when he signed my book. Now, about my mystery man...maybe I'm getting a little too psycho, but I think I might have really screwed up this time. I believe I let my guard down too much. I mean, I sort of got too close, too quick."

"Are you trying to tell me you got laid?"

"Uh, yeah."

"Good for you. I mean seriously, you are old enough. You ain't going to get pregnant. He must have made a huge impression on you because I know you wouldn't have just hopped in bed with him."

"Honestly, it was absolutely wonderful. I don't regret it. But I haven't heard from him since that night. Now, I don't know what to think. I mean, he seemed fine with it. I just thought he would have called or something by now. I don't even know where he lives. He could have a wife and kids and three grandchildren, for all I know. Maybe I jumped in too fast—but I swear, I just didn't want to say no. It felt so *right*. It scared me."

"Maybe it scared him, too. Maybe he doesn't know what to do either. It's bad you don't know much about him. Why don't you ask Cheryl if she knows him? She knows just about everybody around here."

Lily motioned for Cheryl to come over to their table. "Cheryl, do you know a man named Max? He has a Golden Lab."

"Sure. Max Trainor. I know who you're talking about, but I don't know him personally. He mostly keeps to himself. He seems to be a real nice person. He usually comes in here on Wednesdays for a big slice of my fresh apple pie. And he always gets a tall glass of milk with it," Cheryl said. "He'll probably show up tomorrow."

"Please don't say anything to him about me," Lily begged.

"Don't worry. I know nothing, I see nothing, I tell nothing," Cheryl said. "I learned that a long time ago. Besides, if I told everything that I know, I would have to close up the diner and be out on the streets."

"That's the truth," Debra said. "It's a little Peyton Place right here."

Lily walked Debra back to the bookstore, hugged her, and went home. She took a long cool shower, trying not to think of the night with Max. Yet, he shadowed her every thought.

* * *

Earlier that day, down the beach, Max was awakened by Sam nudging him with her cold, wet nose. It was past noon. He reached over to the nightstand and looked at his watch. The morning was gone. He couldn't believe he slept so long. He quickly dressed, combed his hair, and grabbed Sam's leash. *Poor dog,* Max thought. Out the door they went.

As they strolled, he talked to Sam as if she had all the answers. Since they were alone, he figured a private conversation with his best friend would not be considered a loss of sanity. "Sam, I don't know what is going on with me. I've always tried to be a man of integrity with a handful of morals, but last night, I dropped the ball. The problem is, I *wanted* to. Everything felt right. Now, I don't know what to do. Should I wait a few days? If I ask her out, what do I say about last night, if anything? If she only knew... Sam, I can't let her know."

After their walk, Max enjoyed his usual bowl of oatmeal with a few berries, a poached egg, and a slice of wheat toast. Normally his workout began early, but not that day. He had transformed his second bedroom into a fitness room with weight equipment and a treadmill. He refused to become a dumpy old man. However, today, he felt virile and decided to bypass his regular routine.

When the storm passed, he and Sam walked the beach again. The wet, mushy sand sucked at their feet. The damp air brought back a flash of graphic images from a lifetime ago, when he held his buddy in a dank foxhole in Vietnam and watched him die. He saw death come to so many—and even now wondered why not him. Sam, trained to recognize her master's PTSD, slowed her pace and came to a stop. She nudged her head against Max's leg. He knelt down on one knee and hugged his best friend. "I'm OK, Sam." They turned around and walked slowly back home.

Later that night, unable to sleep, he tried to finish reading a book. His attempt to watch television was futile. Being hungry, he munched on chips, not willing to prepare a meal. He was a restless soul all evening. Sam stayed on Max's heels as he paced back and forth. It was obvious to Max that his behavior was affecting Sam when the dog brought her leash to him.

"Sam, surely you don't want to go out again. It's late." Max ruffled Sam's fur.

The dog laid the leash in Max's hand and ran to the door. Reluctantly, he grabbed his jacket and took Sam on her third walk for the day.

Chapter 5

It was past midnight when Lily heard a knock on her front door. She grabbed her .38, slipped into the living room, and peeked out the window. She opened the door when she realized it was Max. He stood there with Sam, not offering an excuse, not saying a word.

"Max?"

He looked down at the gun in her hand and smiled. "I see you are well-prepared."

"Are you OK? Do you know it's in the middle of the night?" Lily asked.

"Can we come in?"

Lily stepped aside. "Sure."

Max sat at the kitchen table while she made a pot of coffee. His unkept appearance was in deep contrast to his meticulous attire a few days ago. His tousled hair and scruffy beard growth actually fascinated Lily. *Oh, I like that rugged look,* she thought.

"Do you want to tell me what's going on, or just let me sit here and guess?" Lily asked.

"I'm really sorry for showing up so late, but I needed to get off the beach. I was taking Sam for a late-night walk when I nearly fell on top of a dead body lying near the water's edge. I turned her over. She had a large gash on the back of her head. Damn it, she wasn't even cold. I didn't see anybody around. The moon was behind the clouds, nearly pitch dark."

"Do you know her?" Lily asked, intrigued by the drama right outside her house.

"Not sure. She looked familiar. Her face was covered in blood, her hair matted with sand. I didn't see any other wounds through her wet clothes. Funny thing, though...she was barefoot. Down the beach, I saw flashing red lights coming my way. I didn't want to be caught up in a mess, so I came here."

Careful not to reveal his past relationship with the dead woman, he held his emotions in check. Seeing Jane, his partner for many years, lying face down, brutally murdered, nearly pushed him to a breaking point.

"Wow, what a story. You know, it could have been a robbery. Gee, it could have been anything. You don't have to leave," Lily said. "Just stay here the rest of the night."

"Thanks. I'll be happy to sleep on the couch. If you can give Sam a quilt, she'll be fine on the floor." He reached down and rubbed Sam's head.

Although the sleeping arrangement seemed strange to Lily, especially after their wild night of sex, she gave Max a sheet, pillow, and quilt for his bed on the couch. She fixed Sam a cozy area near her master. Lily didn't mention their earlier sexual connection. The timing was off, and Max didn't seem to be in a receptive mood. He appeared preoccupied. She didn't press him with questions, sensing he was reluctant to reveal all he knew about the dead woman.

Max didn't sleep. He and Jane had worked several dangerous assignments together in the past. They knew each other very well. They had history: some good, some bad. *But who wanted her dead? And why?*

Still awake at 4 a.m., Lily's thoughts were occupied by the man sleeping on her couch. Not wanting to wake her houseguest, she tiptoed to the bathroom. When she returned, she found Max beneath her sheets, his hand patting her side of the bed. She slipped her nightie down, obliging his unspoken request. He cradled her in his strong arms. It was an intimate moment, holding each other in their nakedness. They soon slept peacefully.

Sam leaped on the bed as the early sunshine brightened the room. Lily stayed in bed, watching Max attempt to not wake her. He wanted to sneak out. He ran his fingers through his untamed hair, bent down, and kissed Lily briefly on the lips, light as a butterfly landing.

"I'm awake." She smiled as she threw back the covers to get out of bed.

"No, no, don't get up. I've imposed on you enough. I've got to get home," Max said. "Can I make it up to you later? Maybe dinner?"

"Sure," she answered. The conversation seemed strained, as if their relationship had reverted to a casual acquaintance.

"OK, I'll get back with you. Thanks again for putting us up for the night."

Max and Sam left. Somewhat aggravated, Lily threw on some clothes. Standing in front of the bathroom mirror, she brushed her hair in a fury. *How is he going to get back with me? He doesn't even have my phone number. I swear, he just ain't right.*

Lily picked up the Eagle Hills Gazette laying just outside her front door. In large print, the headlines scattered details about the deceased woman on the beach last night. An anonymous call to the local police station led them to the scene. No identification found on the body. Cause of death pending.

Lily didn't bother reading the rest of the newspaper. Determined to put Max on the back burner as much as possible, she created a to-do list. She decided he took up too much of her energy. It felt good to cuddle with him, to feel safe in his arms. But he stubbornly kept a wall between them, one so fierce it scared her. Even so, she felt drawn to him. His attitude teetered on arrogance at times. *What is he hiding?*

As she filled the laundry basket, she held up her old, dowdy nightgown. *Oh my, how pitiful.* She left her home on a mission to buy some seductive lingerie, maybe even some alluring bras and panties. She had never purchased anything but cotton panties and cheap bras when Joe was alive. Joe had possessed a large appetite for physical pleasure. Early in the marriage, he had insisted Lily wear no panties, to always be readily available for his needs. She'd never refused him, but that didn't stop him from getting his thrills down the street.

He took her when and where he wanted, with no regard for her feelings or readiness. She learned how to enjoy her own sexual gratification without the emotional connection she craved. Joe couldn't satisfy her body, never her soul.

When he discovered she wouldn't be able to have children, Joe took his passions to other women—*lots* of other women—and Lily adjusted to a loveless and unfulfilled marriage.

She never expected her life to be anything other than what it had been with Joe. She never thought of enjoying complete sexual fulfillment until Max entered her life. She savored every moment, even with all the unanswered questions, and she craved more. *No doubt, wearing tattered, old nightclothes is not the way to seduce a man,* she thought.

She entered the little boutique, Silk & Lace, for the first time since she moved to Eagle Hills. In fact, she had walked past the shop of unmentionables with hardly a glance, never having an inkling of an urge to so much as window-shop the black silk nighties.

A stunning, voluptuous woman with cascading, long, dark hair stood at the counter. "Hello, I'm Beverly. Are you looking for something special today?"

"Maybe...no, thank you. Right now, I just want to look around. I'll probably need your help in a little bit," Lily answered. Her face flushed rosy red, she was so embarrassed. Yet, she was determined to stay and change her lifestyle, even if it meant spending a dollar or two.

Beverly was accustomed to some women feeling shy when they handled the designer panties and bras. She always made an effort to help her customers feel at ease. Little information circulated in the small town about Beverly, except that she lived quite comfortably and drove a BMW. On occasion, she sported her leathers on her Harley, riding with a local motorcycle club. She was an enigma to many of the women in the community—and if the truth be known, they were jealous. She enjoyed her life, not concerned with others' opinions. On the wall behind the counter, she had a poster of the lyrics to Lynyrd Skynyrd's song, "Free Bird." A faint aroma of strawberry incense permeated the shop. There was talk among the gossipers that she was a Woodstock wild child back in the '60s.

Lily picked up a panty that appeared to be missing a bit of cloth. "Beverly, is this supposed to be this way?"

"Yes, dear. You wear it with a full flowing skirt if you want to, well, say... get personal with your lover on an elevator or in a bathroom at a party," Beverly explained.

There was silence.

"Ohh. Oh, my!" Lily whispered.

At that moment, the two women bonded as friends. Beverly knew Lily was far behind with exciting sexual experiences. Lily felt comfortable in asking Beverly about a strong sexual desire with a man she hardly knew.

"My dear, it's very rare these days to enjoy a night of ecstasy with a man who knows how to fulfill a woman's sexual desires. If you have a man like that, you better hang on to him. Don't hold back on pleasing him, either. The more you give, the more he will return. Wait here. I'll be right back," Beverly said. She disappeared into the back room and in a flash, brought out an opened bottle of wine and two small glasses. She filled the glasses and handed one to Lily. They clinked their glasses. "Here's to the men in our lives."

By the time Lily left the Silk & Lace boutique, she had spent two hundred dollars on sexy lingerie, received a wealth of information on the art of sexual arousal, and had an invitation to Beverly's Halloween party. As she walked home, all she thought of was the amazing sensation of Max's body next to hers. Although she had never enjoyed the taste of wine, she found herself feeling very relaxed. At home, she leaned back in her recliner, closed her eyes for just a few minutes, and fell into a deep sleep. When she awoke, darkness covered the house. She didn't think she'd slept but a few minutes. She turned the lamp on. Seeing the time on the wall clock, she realized two hours had slipped by. Still groggy, she undressed and crawled into bed.

For the next two days, Lily submerged herself in reading Brock Savage's novel. She needed a diversion. His book provided that and more. He wrote fiction, yet he weaved some of his conspiracy theories into his stories. Known as very outspoken and a thorn in the side of many politicians, she considered his opinions to be interesting, even if they weren't factual. After finishing the book, she decided to check with Debra for any new books on her shelf. She wasn't going to sit around and wait to see if Max showed up on her doorstep any longer.

At the bookstore, Lily found two more of Savage's novels. Debra was impressed. "I didn't know you liked his books so much, or I'd have told you earlier that I had them on the far shelf," Debra said. "He's staying at the inn for a while. He said he wanted to get the ambience of the small-town life. You know he's from New York. That northern accent is giveaway, and heaven knows, he's eye candy for the women here."

"Well, to me he seems a little uppity, but that might be because of his accent. His theories are insane, but that's what makes a good story," Lily said.

"Did you hear about that dead body on the beach? That's close to your place, right?"

"Yeah, I read about it in the paper. I didn't see anything, though." Lily replied, not mentioning Max. She changed the conversation quickly. "Do you know a woman named Beverly, who owns that boutique a few doors down from Cheryl's Diner?"

"I know who she is, but I don't know her personally. She runs with different crowds. I've seen several limos parked in front of her house at one time, and then I've noticed at least a dozen motorcycles parked there. I did hear a rumor that back in the day she hooked up with a band member of the Stones. I don't know if that's true or not. She sure ain't needy."

"I went in there a couple of days ago and bought a few things. She seems to be very nice. She invited me to her Halloween party, but I don't know if I'll go," Lily explained.

"Oh, good grief, Lily; you'd better go. That's a chance of a lifetime. You will meet all kinds of people, and for sure, have a great time. You'll mingle with the cream of the crop and the down and dirty. I'm jealous!"

"OK, I'll think about it. It's this Friday, I believe. Maybe I'll go just out of curiosity, and the fact that I'll have to report back to you."

They giggled as Lily paid for the books and left. Feeling a hunger pang, she stopped in the diner for her favorite meal, spaghetti. Cheryl's recipe for spaghetti sauce was one of the best kept secrets in Eagle Hills. Many tried to bribe her and several attempts were made to duplicate it, but they all failed.

At first, she didn't see him when she sat down at the counter. While taking Lily's order, Cheryl kept winking at her. "Cheryl, is something wrong with your eye?"

"No," Cheryl mumbled. Grinning, she rolled her eyes and tilted her head toward the other end of the counter.

Lily turned to look; Max sat four stools down, on her right. He hadn't noticed her either. *Oh! This is Wednesday, and he's here for the pie,* she thought.

Suddenly, she jumped. "Ooh!" She'd felt Sam's cold nose on her ankle.

27

She reached down and rubbed the dog's head. Lily wished she could just leave unannounced, but now that Sam spied her, she was stuck. She decided to just ignore Max; maybe he wouldn't see her.

After savoring the last bite of his pie, Max got up to leave. Sam led him straight to the woman he'd spent the last few days trying to forget. He tapped Lily on the shoulder. "It's good to see you again. I was hoping to run into you, since I don't have your phone number. I didn't want to just show up on your doorstep without warning again," he said.

Lily smiled. "Glad to see you too. I thought maybe you disappeared."

"I owe you a dinner. How about tonight? That is, if you're free?"

They made dinner plans, and Lily gave him her phone number. But when she got home, she was angry at herself for doing it. She wanted to erase the last several days, but she was drawn to him every time she saw him. She tried to convince herself that he wasn't worth another minute of her attention. Yet, the memory of their night together overshadowed her reasons to forget him.

Promptly at five o'clock, Max knocked on her door. He had made reservations at Big Al's Seafood Hut, one of nicer restaurants on the beach. The walk was a little longer, but well worth the time. The hostess seated them next to a large window to enjoy the beautiful scenery of crashing waves against the reef. Unfamiliar with the menu, she allowed Max to place the order of lobster with drawn butter, steamed asparagus, a big salad, and a dry white wine. She felt a little nervous, knowing her behavior became overtly amorous when she drank wine. She figured she could (surely) act like an adult in public, so she graciously accepted the chardonnay. Dinner was delicious, full of flavor. Max popped a succulent bite of lobster into his mouth. She smiled as a drop of creamy butter beaded on his bottom lip.

"Here, let me get that," she said as she leaned in. She gently wiped the liquid, slowly licking her finger, using her tongue in the most sensuous manner Max had ever envisioned.

Not expecting such a public display, he glanced around the room. Fortunately, no one was interested in her show of excitement. He knew then he needed to take her behind closed doors, and quickly. As Lily's glass emptied for the second time, she appeared even more relaxed, yet bold. By the time he paid the bill and tipped the waiter, he was hell-bound to get back to her place. He did not want her to bring attention to his presence. He slipped his arm around her shoulders as they walked, and she gave him a quick kiss on his neck. He figured, surely she wasn't intoxicated; she was just showing a happy state of mind.

As soon as they entered her cottage, she stepped in front of him, pushing him against the living room wall. She reached up to pull his head down, placing her mouth on his waiting lips as she explored the hardness in his pants. He loved her touch.

"You have become my fountain of youth," Max whispered. "Where have you been all these years?"

No answer.

Slowly, he slipped his hand beneath her blouse and unclasped her black lacy bra. She moaned as she took his hand away. He knew she wanted to be in control of their night. She led him to the couch, pushing him down. She stood in front of him, slowly removing her blouse and bra. He reached for her supple breasts, wanting to bury his head between them. She shook her head. "No," she whispered. Her seduction was overwhelming.

She knelt down, unzipped his pants, and released his shaft. Still, she would not allow him to touch her. She leaned over, opening her mouth. Surprisingly artful in her technique, he cried out in his lust for her. He watched as her tongue captured a drop of his nectar. "Take me, Babe." Max murmured. He was rising to the brink quickly. She raised her head and smiled. She straddled him, easing herself down on his throbbing manhood. She let out a soft sigh. She rocked in a slow rhythm atop of him. He couldn't stand it any longer. He took her like a wild animal. He quivered as he unleashed his juice. He was being controlled by this sexual being, and he loved it. She joined him, climbing to the peak of her desire. They held on to each other, riding the waves of ecstasy, leaving both of them spent.

They straightened their clothes in silence. She leaned against his chest as they remained on the couch, trying to make sense of what was going on.

"Would you like something to drink?" Lily asked. "A glass of water?"

"Yeah, I would appreciate that."

Lily hadn't bothered to put her panties back on. Max watched her firm derriere sway as she went into the kitchen. He hated himself. He wished his life was different. He couldn't keep up this façade forever... Or could he? Being with her gave rise to a potential threat. When she returned with the water, he stood at her front door.

"I'm sorry, Lily. I need to go now. Please try to be patient with me. You are an amazing woman." Once again, Max made an unexplained exit from Lily's arms. His legs shaky, his body drained, he wished their night had lasted even longer. Yet, he knew he would be putting her in a dangerous situation. "I'm sorry, Honey. I will call you." He left.

Lily stood there holding the glass of water, fighting the urge to throw it at the door as it closed. Those last words pissed her off. It had been a night of fulfilled fantasies. *Whatever it is that makes him run away keeps him a prisoner,* she thought. *Damn him.* She gathered her clothes off the floor and went to bed. Staring at the ceiling, her anger increased as she relived their passionate desires. She finally burst into tears. *I don't understand. Am I doing something wrong again? One minute he's all over me, and the next he acts like he can't get away from me fast enough. Sometimes it seems he wants to confide in me, but then he stops cold. I just don't know what to do!* She closed her eyes, tears still streaming.

Chapter 6

The next morning, Max bought the *Eagle Hills Gazette* from the news-stand at the end of the pier during his mid-morning walk with Sam. Not bothering to look at the headlines, he folded the eight-page newspaper under his arm and carried it home. It was a crisp October morning; the sun shone brightly, bringing warmth to the chilly day. He sat outside on his small patio. As the steam rose from his cup of coffee on the little table, he unfolded the newspaper. Seeing a picture of Jane unnerved him. Reading the latest information caused him to knock his cup over, spilling the coffee over the article. "Damn."

Immediately, Max's thoughts ran rampant. *Why was she here? Who sent her?*

Anger took its place over the frustration Max felt. He stood at the railing, grabbed his empty cup, and threw it far into a thicket beside his house. *Damn it to hell,* he thought. He only had one cup left in his cupboard.

"Sam, go get my cup," he ordered, pointing to the clump of weeds.

The dog raced to obey her master's command. However, instead of bringing back the cup, she continued to stare into the brush, whining. Max figured there might be a critter or a snake scaring Sam, so he walked down to her.

"What's wrong, girl? You don't scare easy," he said, squatting down to get a better look.

Max spread the tall weeds apart, then reached down and collected a Kel-Tec PMR-30 pistol, one of the few that uses .22 WMR ammunition. He quickly looked around to see if anyone was nearby, then covered the gun with both hands and walked slowly back to his house. Once inside, he locked the door. He sat at the kitchen table to examine the handgun. He was familiar with the model from the time he spent in the military. Foreign intelligence agencies often used this type of gun; it's fast, cheap, low damage, and has pinpoint accuracy. This one was loaded. The serial number on the gun was marred, but still readable. He called an old friend in the ATF and asked him to check on the serial number without going through the regular processing. *One thing's for sure, I'm not putting it back where I found it,* he thought. He placed the weapon inside a pillowcase and laid it between a set of sheets in the fitness room closet.

Sam followed Max like a shadow the rest of the day. Max felt uneasy. *Were the bullets meant for him? Did he or she plant the gun to return later?* Scattered questions raced through his thoughts. His phone rang twice, but he ignored the calls. Slightly paranoid—or maybe just overly cautious—he stayed inside, with the shades pulled tightly and his loaded Beretta .380 nearby. He wanted to call Lily, but didn't. He couldn't involve her in his find. He didn't have any answers. Always approached in the past by a runner in public places, detailed instructions provided him with a sort of safety net. If danger became imminent, he moved to a different location. *I'm getting old, and I'm getting tired of disappearing at the drop of a hat. I want my life back. I've found a woman I want to spend time with. I care deeply for her,* he thought. *I wish I could confide in her, explain why I seem to run away from her. At least I have Sam.*

* * *

Lily was thoroughly engrossed in the front page of the newspaper. The dead woman on the beach had a name: Jane Lawson. The article described her as an aide to Senator John Butcher, who headed up the Senate Committee on Foreign Relations. The local police were treating her death as a homicide. Additional details would be provided when available.

"Hmmm, well, that's very interesting. Wonder what she was doing here," Lily said aloud. "Max certainly looked fidgety talking about it." She mulled over that night he came over, recalling how nervously he had behaved when telling her about the corpse.

Lily was surprised to get a phone call from Joanie that evening, and even more surprised when Joanie said she was coming for a visit. They chatted for nearly an hour, finally agreeing on Saturday, hoping the warm days of Indian summer would give Joanie a chance to enjoy the autumn colors. As best friends since kindergarten, they had suffered through teenage heartbreaks together, kept each other's dark secrets, and supported each other during times of loneliness. Early in Lily's marriage to Joe, Joanie told Lily she deserved someone better than him. At that time, Lily wasn't aware of his philandering. She thought Joanie had betrayed her. For a short time, the two acted cool toward each other. As in all small towns, Lily eventually discovered her husband kept mistresses at various times during their long marriage. But after the police came to her home with the news that Joe died in the arms of one of his women, it was Joanie who comforted her through the embarrassing mess.

Joanie had grown up quick and hard in the rough side of Hoggville, Tennessee. At the age of seven, she witnessed a stabbing in front of the home she shared with her aunt and uncle, along with five younger cousins. By the time she graduated eighth grade, she was accustomed to hearing late-night gunshots echo in the holler. In high school, she blossomed into a beautiful young girl who never lacked for a date. The friendship between Joanie and Lily was an odd combination. While Lily strolled through life in agreement with whatever came along, Joanie proved ready to fight for what she needed. They complimented each other's personalities.

As Lily looked at the calendar on the kitchen wall, she noticed the day she'd penciled in a note about Beverly's party. It was on Friday, only a few days away. She needed to find a costume. *Too late to order one*, she thought. She called Debra for advice. Luckily, a little party supply store nearby carried a variety of costumes. Wasting no more time, Lily hurried to the store.

Entering Michele's Party Shop, she was amazed by the array of supplies in multiple themes and colors, something for every event and holiday. She found several aisles of decorations and party favors in attractive displays. At the far end, covering the entire wall, hung an assortment of child and adult costumes. It didn't take long to find one; she quickly chose a sexy SWAT

33

costume, complete with black fishnet stockings and knee-high boots. It also included a badge and a hat. She took the merchandise to the counter, smiling.

"Did you find everything you need?" Michele asked, as she tallied the price.

"Yes, thank goodness. I'm surprised you still have some left," Lily answered. "I'd forgotten about a party I'm attending in a few days. My friend Debra, at the bookstore, told me to come here."

"Well, I'm awfully glad you found us. Are you going to Beverly's party? I mean, it's the only one around here," Michele said. "It's usually pretty quiet here on Halloween, except up at her house. I'm sure you'll have a good time. She's a wonderful hostess."

Lily paid for her merchandise, thanked Michele, and left as a satisfied customer. Now, the party occupied her thoughts instead of Max. Yet, she couldn't help but wonder if he would be there.

Lily looked forward to Beverly's Halloween party, her first real party since moving to Eagle Hills. She figured if Max didn't show up, she could still have a good time. The day of the party dragged on as she waited to play dress-up with her costume. Finally, late that afternoon, Lily spread her outfit out on the bed. She had tried it on earlier; not only did it fit, it showed off her curves. *I don't look too bad for an old woman,* she thought. *Maybe I can surprise Max—that is, if I ever get him in bed again.* She grinned. *I can't believe I even thought that.*

The party started at eight. Although it was only a short distance to Beverly's house, Lily decided to drive anyway. She felt a bit embarrassed to be walking the streets wearing a SWAT uniform that could be misconstrued as a lady of the night in role-playing gear. *That's all I'd need, for the police to pick me up,* she thought.

As she parked her SUV among the Bentleys and the Porsches at Beverly's home, she noticed a large line of Harleys, Indians, and several Hondas. She wasn't driving the only American made car there, at least; she counted four others. Lily slipped through the maze of cars and up to the brightly lit walkway leading to the front door. Pumpkins, haystacks, and scarecrows adorned the yard. Hanging from the tree limbs were massive white webs with huge, black spiders, flashing red LEDs in their eyes. Lily stepped up on the porch to be met by a tall vampire robot that raised its arm saying, "May I help you?"

Lily let out a squeal. There were a few guests standing on the porch with their drinks, oblivious to her reaction. With the music blaring, she knew the party was in full force. She went inside. Immediately, a server wearing only a thin loincloth offered her a drink. She caught herself staring at his massive biceps and smooth, tanned chest.

"Uh, what do you recommend?" she asked. *Oh, you are such a boy toy. Oh my!*

"We have several popular drinks, including Dracula's Kiss, Witches' Brew, and Zombies," the server said. "For you... Might I suggest a Transylvania Iced Tea?"

The handsome young man handed her the tall glass of tea. Lily scanned the room, seeing some of the guests wearing masks, hiding their identities. Free to behave in an alternative fashion, Lily considered their actions in poor taste.

She felt a tap on her shoulder and turned around to face Beverly, dressed in a genie costume. The gold camisole accented her impressive cleavage. She sparkled all over, the sequined waistband on the sheer, glittering harem pants emphasizing her long legs. Tiny gold slippers completed her outfit.

"I'm so glad you came," Beverly said, giving Lily a brief hug. "Enjoy yourself. If you see unfamiliar faces, there's no need for introductions. Just jump right in and feel comfortable. Those who have masks are content to be incognito, if you know what I mean."

"Thank you."

Beverly disappeared into the crowd, leaving Lily standing at the doorway into another large room. She took a sip of her tea and joined the party. Black linen tablecloths covered several round tables, the seating adorned by orange chair covers. The only light came from lanterns strategically placed to emit moving shadows. The spirit of Halloween was everywhere. Music played throughout the house; "Monster Mash" bounced off the walls as Lily sipped her drink.

At the buffet, she sampled a sandwich that was shaped like a finger, oozing a blood like substance. Actually, it was quite tasty. Her glass of tea was nearly empty when she accepted another. She engaged in several small group conversations with people she didn't know. It seemed to her that the music got louder as the night went by. By midnight, she was a dancing fool, tasting another freedom she had never experienced. While searching for the bathroom, she opened a walk-in closet door.

"Uh oh!" Lily said. It was a vision she'd never expected in all her recent wild dreams. In front of her was a genie, bent over, receiving the mighty weapon of Evan the Assassin.

Beverly grabbed a coat off a hanger, covering her nakedness. She laughed. "Oh, hi, Lily. I would like you to meet the legendary Evan, AKA Brock Savage."

Brock didn't bother to hide his large asset. "Ah, Lily. I think we've met before...at the bookstore, I believe."

"Oh God, I'm so sorry. I was looking for a bathroom," Lily said. She backed out of the closet, shut the door, and burst out laughing.

She didn't see Evan, AKA Brock, for the rest of the night. It was a relief; she had no idea what to say to him without embarrassing herself. She did talk to Beverly at the end of the night, and thanked her for a wonderful time. Beverly had been confirmed to be a gracious host to all her guests—but no doubt, she'd given special attention to Evan the Assassin.

The party wound down and guests began to leave, so Lily was able to find her car easily. When she clicked to unlock the car door, a man grabbed her shoulders and pushed her up against the car. Suddenly she was staring at the Joker. His disturbing clown makeup made it impossible to recognize him. Despite the cool night air, he reeked of cigar smoke.

"Be careful, little lady. You're being watched," the supervillain said in a gruff voice. Then, he released her and disappeared into the darkness.

Chapter 7

Shaken and in tears, Lily wasted no time getting home. She ran inside and locked the door. Afraid to turn a light on, she stumbled around in the dark until she fell into her bed, fully clothed. Although tired and still a bit woozy from the alcohol, she never closed her eyes. Every sound she heard seemed loud and intentional. The man dressed as the Joker had really frightened her. As daylight crept through the shades and closed curtains, her body sank in exhaustion. She finally got out of bed and sat down at the kitchen table, intent on drinking a pot of black coffee.

It wasn't even eight a.m., still early. She thought about going back to bed, but knew she would just toss and turn. *Sleep is not on the menu today*, Lily thought. She looked forward to having Joanie come for a short visit. Lily needed some hometown connection, and she needed to talk to her best friend. She knew Joanie would believe her when she said that the Joker grabbed her in the middle of the night and spouted a dire warning.

Lily spent the day cleaning the extra bedroom, putting fresh sheets on the bed and clean towels in the bathroom. She even placed a mint on a pillow, knowing Joanie would get a kick out of her hotel accommodations.

Around four, Lily heard the roar of a motorcycle in front of the cottage. Instead of waiting, Lily ran outside to greet her best friend. She hardly gave Joanie a chance to get off her Harley. "Oh, Joanie, I'm so happy you're here! I just can't believe you rode all the way out of the holler." They hugged.

"Whew! I didn't think it would be such a long ride, but I did it," Joanie said, while taking her helmet off. "I'm telling you, I thought Tennessee boasted some wild, winding roads, but North Carolina tops it. There are some hairpin curves that made my curly hair stand up straight."

Once inside, Lily showed Joanie the guest bedroom and helped her put away her clothes. Joanie filled Lily in on all the gossip back home. By the time they had talked about the marriages, divorces, deaths, and births, it had turned to dusk outside. Because Joanie had never seen the ocean, they walked down to the water's edge. The moon made a rippling, glowing path through the ocean's waves. They stood silent for several minutes, admiring the beauty of the night and appreciating the true meaning of friendship. It became a special time for the two women: a memory captured, sisterhood forever.

"I thought we could go out and get a bite to eat. There's a diner close by. Lock up your bike. We can walk," Lily suggested.

"Sounds good to me. I need to walk this stiffness out anyway."

While Lily locked her door, Joanie secured her bike, and they walked to Cheryl's Diner. It was nearly empty inside. Cheryl was wiping the counters, preparing to close up soon.

"Cheryl, this is my best friend, Joanie, from my hometown. Is it too late to get a sandwich? I didn't realize it was closing time," Lily said.

"Come on in and sit down. It won't take a minute. I'll fix you up with a roast beef sandwich and chips," Cheryl said. "I've put away most of today's menu."

"That sounds great. Thanks," Lily said.

Cheryl nodded to Joanie. "Nice to meet you, Joanie."

"Same here," Joanie replied.

Cheryl brought the food out. "Here you go, ladies. It's on the house."

They thanked Cheryl and asked her to sit down with them in the booth. The conversation was general and polite for a few minutes, but Lily couldn't wait anymore.

"Y'all, I'm going to bust if I don't talk to somebody. Since we're the only ones in here now, this is a good time as any," Lily declared.

"OK, we're all ears," Joanie said.

Lily began telling the story of her attack. "I went to a Halloween party at a friend's house last night; her name is Beverly. I'm sure you know her,

Cheryl. It was a great party: good food, music, and lots of people. It broke up near midnight. When I started to open my car door, a man grabbed me. He said to be careful, that I was being watched. Then he just turned around and left me standing there, scared to death. I jumped in my car and took off."

"Do you know who he is?" Cheryl asked.

"No. He was dressed as the Joker," Lily said.

Joanie burst out laughing. Cheryl covered her mouth, trying not to laugh.

"Hey, that's not fair! I don't know what's going on, and you're laughing at me," Lily fussed. "A big help you two are! I need advice. This is serious!"

"Listen...it could've been a drunk who was just too much into his role-playing, not meaning any harm," Cheryl suggested. "I wouldn't take it so seriously. Sometimes after her parties, there's been a few come in here still in their costumes. They pretend to be everything from Star Wars characters to Little Red Riding Hood to the Grim Reaper. It isn't just at Halloween that she has dress-up parties."

"Now if something else happens, then I believe I'd be concerned. But for now, leave it alone," Joanie said. "Besides, I've got your back." Joanie had a way about her, making others feel at ease. She also had a license to carry concealed, and Lily knew for a fact she was a damn good shot.

Lily felt a bit relieved. "Maybe I've blown it out of proportion, but it really creeped me out. I'm not used to some man messing with me like that. I mean, he could have been a lunatic, even a serial killer or a kidnapper. Then what?"

"Oh crap, Lily. If somebody abducted you, they'd let you go when it turned daylight and they found out nobody was going to pay a ransom," Joanie said.

"OK, I give up. You two are just awful," Lily said. "Let's all go for a drink at Ernie's. I'm buying."

"I appreciate it, but I have to finish a ton of paperwork before closing. Go on, have a good time," Cheryl said. "I've really enjoyed the conversation, though. Maybe next time."

When Lily and Joanie left, Cheryl locked the door and turned out the lights. Her home was just a few steps away: she still lived in the back of the restaurant. Life hadn't been easy for Cheryl. She had learned at an early age to make do with what she got. She felt grateful for the little place she called home. She spent her youth in foster homes, married in her teens, and divorced two years later with a disabled child who succumbed to pneumonia and died at the age of three. It was all downhill after that.

Lily and Joanie walked into Ernie's during a very crowded darts tournament. Luckily, they found two seats at the counter. Joanie enjoyed the atmosphere; she'd worked as a bartender several times during her life. She enjoyed the patrons, plus the money paid the bills. She never depended on her beauty for tips, though. She worked hard, determined to always be an asset. She didn't need a computer to show her how to mix a drink. Very talented, she entertained the customers with bar tricks and bottle juggling.

"Ernie, I'd like you to meet a good friend of mine from Tennessee. Her name is Joanie," Lily said.

Ernie smiled and shook Joanie's hand. "Nice to meet you."

Joanie nodded politely, saying nothing.

"Joanie, Ernie is one of the best bartenders in North Carolina. At least, that's what he brags," Lily said.

"What can I get you ladies?" Ernie asked, placing a coaster in front of each of them.

"I'll have a bourbon on the rocks, please," Joanie said.

"Me too," Lily chimed in.

"I'll be right with you," Ernie said, as he fixed the drinks.

When Joanie excused herself to the ladies' room, Ernie leaned close to Lily. "Your friend, is she single?"

"Yes. Why? Are you interested?"

"I might be. You won't give me the time of day. You can't say I ain't tried. So, will you put in a good word for me?"

"Sure, Ernie. But you need to know, she doesn't take any bull from anybody. Oh, and by the way, she can give you a run on being the best bartender," Lily said. "She could teach you a thing or two. That I can guarantee."

Ernie snickered. "Hmm. I'll keep that in mind."

When Joanie came back to the bar, Ernie soon became overwhelmed with the burst of business from the darts players and didn't get a chance to flirt with her.

"Ernie's interested in you," Lily whispered. "He asked me to put in a good word for him. He's a good guy, as far as I know."

"Really? Well, he sure is easy on the eyes. Single?" Joanie asked. "You know I don't mess with married men, not since that idiot from Knoxville years ago. Once was enough."

"Yes, he's single. He's been in a few long-term relationships in the past, but nothing's been going on recently," Lily explained. "He's safe."

The women finished their drinks, and Lily waved at Ernie, intending to pay the tab. He waved back and gave her a thumbs up, meaning the drinks were on the house. They giggled like schoolgirls on the way back to the cottage. It was one more freedom that Lily had discovered in Eagle Hills: to be herself in public.

"That was fun, girlfriend. You've got some nice people here. I've been kinda worried about you, but you're doing just fine," Joanie said.

"Yeah, I think so. I've really been trying not to be a recluse and to get out more. You know I didn't have much of a social life when I was married. So it's still hard for me to let loose with a crowd, unless I've been drinking. Oh yeah, I have to tell you about a drink I had at that party. They called it Transylvania Iced Tea. It knocked my socks off."

"Oh, for heaven's sake, Lily, that was probably a Long Island Iced Tea. Yeah, it will set you straight, and it doesn't take much. I've fixed a many of them at fancy parties."

When they got back to Lily's cottage, they found the front door ajar.

"Joanie, wait a minute. I'm sure I locked the door when we left. At least, I *think* I'm sure," Lily said. "Should I call the police?"

"No, not yet." Joanie pulled her Smith & Wesson M&P .22 out of her handbag. She took the safety off and said, "Slip your hand through that crack and turn on the light. Do it slowly."

Lily reached in and flipped the overhead light switch on. Then they stepped inside. They checked every room, including the closets. Nothing was moved, damaged, or stolen.

"I guess I didn't lock the door. Maybe a breeze pushed it open," Lily said. "I'm glad you were with me. I wouldn't have come in if you hadn't been here. I checked my nightstand drawer and my .38 is still there. You were right; there was no sense in calling the police. I guess I'm letting my imagination run away with me."

"I could have sworn you locked that door, but we were gabbing away. Oh, well, everything's here, so don't worry about it. Guess I'll have to keep an eye on you after all." Joanie put her pistol on her nightstand. "Honey, I'm really worn out, so if you don't care, I'm going to bed."

"Me too. Get a good night's rest. See you in the morning," Lily said. "Love ya, girl."

"Love you too. If you need me, just holler. Oh, and thanks for the mint. I feel like I'm staying at the Hilton."

As soon as Lily lay down, her phone rang. It was Max. He asked if she would like a late-night visitor. She declined, giving Joanie as her excuse. She wanted badly to be with him again, but not on his whim every time. Max asked her to go to Ernie's the following night to hear a new band and extended the invitation to Joanie as well. They planned to meet at 7 p.m. in front of the bar. After they hung up, Lily curled up in her bed, wishing his arms were around her. Her feelings were confusing, intense, and swinging from one extreme to the other; sometimes, she couldn't stand him, and other times, she wanted him so much she couldn't think straight. Her dreams that night were disturbing. She kept reliving the scene with the Joker, waking up in a sweat. Her inner self nagged her, insisting it was not a prank, and he was not a random drunk.

* * *

Max felt disappointed when Lily declined his self-invitation. He realized he was taking a chance calling so late. He needed Lily but not for what she thought. The frustration brought on by Jane's death, plus finding the loaded gun, caused him to panic. Sam stayed close to her master as he paced the floors. It had been a long time since Max had become engulfed in a full-blown PTSD attack. Finally coming out of it somewhat, he sat down on his couch, put his trembling hands over his face, and cried.

"It's OK, Sam. I'll be all right," he said, giving the dog a hug. "Maybe it was a good thing I didn't go over to Lily's tonight."

Max crawled in bed and turned out his light, then settled on his back, staring into the darkness. He knew he was safe because Sam was there. Finally, sleep came.

Chapter 8

The following day, Lily took Joanie to several shops in the area, including the lingerie boutique. Beverly didn't hesitate to break out the wine glasses. Lily didn't mention the scene in the walk-in closet. She didn't want to embarrass Beverly. But to Lily's surprise, Beverly brought up the sexcapade. It seemed that Brock and Beverly had kept a yearly tryst for a long time—usually during Halloween, but always in costume.

"Oh, Brock is one of my dearest friends. He's an odd character, to some, but that's what makes him exciting. He's one of the most loyal friends I have. When he worked for the government, he was privy to a lot of secret missions that none of us will ever hear about. I hated it when he retired early. Maybe he knew more than he should have. For sure, we'll never know," Beverly said. "We're just good friends who enjoy an occasional exciting roll in the hay. And trust me, he's *very* good at what he does. He lights my fire every time. I'm sure you know what I mean."

Joanie hardly said a word, clearly dumbfounded to hear such a casual conversation about sex. The townspeople of Hoggville hadn't changed with the times; the attitudes there remained stuck in the past, as if it was fifty years ago. Even the word *sex* was never spoken in public, and certainly not in mixed company. Sexual encounters were usually kept secret. Yet, it seemed the word always got out eventually, and the gossipers embellished the story. Joanie had been the subject of the week many times. Whether it was true or not, no one knew or cared.

Joanie abruptly changed the subject. "Lily, did you tell Beverly about what happened with the Joker?"

Lily repeated the story. To her surprise, Beverly knew who was underneath the costume. When Beverly told her it was Senator John Butcher, Lily wasn't impressed.

"I don't know the man, never met him in my life," Lily said. "And I sure don't want to now. He scared me to death."

"Let me tell you about the senator. He's been married three times, and out of those marriages, there are five *legitimate* children. His present wife is named Sheri, I think. I try to keep all the names straight. She's lasted longer than the others; she's a registered nurse and professor at the community college, teaching in the nurse practitioner program. He has two other children by some woman who works in his office and often accompanies him to events. I've seen her at a distance, but I've never met her. He parties a lot but has his finger in every covert military operation," Beverly said. "Oh, and he was a prisoner of war. He's a bit quirky and a prankster at that. You just have to take him with a grain of salt. But if he tells you something, you need to listen. He's not stupid."

After a short discussion, Beverly agreed with Joanie that maybe he was just drunk and behaving foolishly. Still, Lily felt uneasy.

Before the two women said their good-byes to Beverly, Joanie bought several unmentionables and a sheer red nightie that left little to the imagination. Back at the cottage, Lily told Joanie about the plans she'd made for the evening. Joanie became excited when she learned she was going to meet this mystery man named Max. She was secretly thrilled that she would be seeing Ernie again, too. Maybe this time, she would find out more about that sexy bartender.

Since they hadn't eaten lunch and it was near dinner time, Lily ordered a pizza from Bob's Pizza Parlor. Bob was known for his fast delivery; his motto was, if it took more than forty-five minutes, the pizza was free. Everybody liked Bob; he was a friendly sort of guy who loved to tell jokes, a hard worker, and a family man. When Lily first moved to Eagle Hills, Bob refused her money on her first order. He said it was a welcome pizza, sort of a tradition for new customers.

The women forgot their manners as they ate the super loaded pizza. They hurried, needing to get dressed and leave by 6:30. Since Joanie couldn't bring many clothes in the bag on her bike, she borrowed a skirt from Lily. Rarely did Lily wear a dress or skirt after moving to Eagle Hills. But since Joanie had decided to dress up, Lily donned a loose flowing skirt and a low-cut peasant blouse. She considered wearing a thong but it felt uncomfortable, so she decided to go commando. *It doesn't matter; no one will know anyway.* Unlike the past when Joe demanded she not wear panties, this time she felt sexy.

The ladies were right on time, standing in front of the bar when Max came. Lily briefly introduced him to Joanie. Then, they went inside. They each took a stool at the counter because all the booths were filled. Ernie wiped his hands on a bar towel and took their orders, unable to take his eyes off of Joanie. There was an obvious mutual attraction going on. When a booth became empty, Max and Lily took it. Joanie, however, chose to stay seated at the bar so she could talk to Ernie. She learned that Ernie was a biker too, which gave him a ton of brownie points. She never dated anyone who didn't ride.

Over in the booth, Max apologized to Lily about calling so late the night before. He didn't give a lengthy explanation, just admitted that he had her on his mind. Since she'd started to think she was a one-night stand, Lily appreciated his honesty. Max held her hand. She listened closely as he spoke about when he had moved to Eagle Hills—but she was more impressed by his romantic gesture than his words.

Laughter filled the air in the small establishment. Joanie challenged Ernie with one of her famous bar tricks, and Ernie failed miserably. By closing time, Joanie was behind the bar mixing them each an Old Fashioned.

As Max and Lily got up to leave, Lily asked Joanie if she was ready to go. Joanie looked at Ernie. He smiled.

"Lily, you two go on without me. I'm going to stay here for a while and help Ernie close up," Joanie said. "Besides, I have to finish my drink."

"Don't worry, she's in good hands," Ernie said, putting his arm around Joanie.

Lily and Max took their time walking back to her place. They took a stroll down on the pier, leaned on the railing to watch to rolling waves, and savored the sea air. The dim lighting from the lampposts gave just enough illumination for safety. They didn't talk; they didn't need to. Max stood behind Lily and wrapped his arms around her, protecting her from a sudden brisk spray. He wanted to tell her about his past, but he couldn't. She wanted to tell him how much he meant to her, but she didn't. Both were fighting to relinquish their walls of self-protection.

The warmth of their bodies brought on an exciting desire from Max. He gently kissed the back of her neck. Then, his hands rose under her jacket and cupped her breasts, squeezing gently. She felt his hardness as he pressed against her rear. She wanted him to take her right there, right then. His thoughts were the same—and it would have happened, if they had not heard the voices of others approaching.

They left the pier in a hurry. Lily was anxious to get home to continue the touching, feeling, and more. Max had other ideas. As they came upon the lifeguard shack, he took her hand and led her up the steps. The door was locked.

"Let's go, before we get caught up here," she whispered, pulling away.

"No, wait, let me try something," he said. He slipped his credit card through the crack between the door and frame, then pushed down on the rusty bolt while twisting the knob. It released with a loud click, and he opened the door.

"But Max..." she protested.

"Shhh. Don't make so much noise," he said. "Come on in here. Let me show you something."

Lily felt like she was in high school, sneaking around to make out with her boyfriend. But this time, she was going to enjoy the passion of a man whose raw, primal lust demanded to be satisfied. With her back to him, he slipped her skirt up to find her round ass bare. He smiled and unzipped his pants, releasing his hard shaft. He bent her over the small counter and grabbed her hips. The thrill of having sex in the tiny shack on the beach created a quickly mounting excitement. Lily gasped as he filled her; it was a different feeling, a different position, one she had never experienced. They climbed to their peak and let go. It was quick, but it was good. He leaned over her, his strength drained, as she collapsed on the counter.

"Are you OK, babe?" Max asked.

"Oh," she said. "You are amazing."

They quickly rearranged their clothes, peeked outside to see if the coast was clear, and hurried back to Lily's cottage. When they got to the patio, he whirled her around and took her in his arms. They laughed and held each other for a moment. It was the most exciting night of Lily's life—again. Max felt on top of the world. For the first time, neither cared about what tomorrow would bring. Their joy was in the present, and they were happy.

"I'll say good night to you now. I hope you've had as much fun as I have," Max said. "You're very special to me, I hope you know that."

"Thank you for everything. I can't stop smiling," Lily said. She reached up and kissed him. It was a sweet kiss, a kiss of complete satisfaction. "You're special to me too." This time, she didn't question her response to this man who had entered and exited her life multiple times, without any hint of stability. She felt adventurous, willing to take a chance on the unknown. It was about time.

As he left, she unlocked her door and went inside. Soon, she heard a motorcycle pull up and stop. After several minutes, she peered out the window to see Ernie sitting on his bike and Joanie straddling him. Their movements were obvious. Apparently, Joanie was enjoying her night also. Lily wanted to watch all the action, but felt like a voyeur. For a split second, Lily wanted to flicker the porch light like Joanie was a teenager late for curfew, just to be mischievous. Reluctantly, she turned away and waited for Joanie to come in. Another twenty minutes passed before Joanie walked into the kitchen.

"Did you have a good time with Ernie tonight?" Lily asked.

"I sure did," Joanie said. "He's got a real nice bike."

"I'll bet he does." Lily giggled.

"You spied on me, didn't you? I thought I saw you looking out the window. Shame on you."

"Hey, girlfriend, you two were right out in public. It was a free show. I'm glad you got laid. Now you won't be so cranky."

"Well, you're acting right pleasant yourself. Did Max give you anything tonight?"

Lily snickered. "If I tell you this, you better never tell a living soul."

Joanie crossed her heart. "OK, I swear. Now spill it!"

Lily told her about sneaking into the lifeguard shack. "We had the most exciting sex. I think it's called a quickie."

The two women burst out laughing, both happy and content. It was late, but they weren't sleepy.

"Do you have anything in your fridge to eat? What about the rest of that pizza? I'm starved," Joanie said. "Is your cupboard bare?"

"I've got a little ice cream left, in a pint in the freezer. It's at least two months old. Or I can warm up that pizza; there's a few slices left. I guess we need to go to the grocery store tomorrow. But for now, what do you want? The pizza or the ice cream?" Lily asked.

"Save the ice cream. That's for when we're sad. I think we're both in happy moods, so let's eat the pizza."

After finishing their late-night snack, the euphoria wore off and they went to bed. They had no trouble falling asleep. However, down the beach, sleep didn't come as easily for Max. He was dealing with an intruder.

Chapter 9

Max didn't hesitate to take the safety off his gun when he awoke with Sam nudging him and whimpering in the middle of the night. He got out of bed slowly and silently, then crept over to stand at the doorway into the living room. He assumed the beam of light coming through his front window was a flashlight. Sam stood perfectly still, waiting for Max's command to attack.

Someone turned the knob on the front door. Max readied his gun to meet the stranger. He had locked the door earlier, but he knew better than anyone how easy it was to flip a lock. Max's heart raced. Sam, unable to remain quiet, swiftly lunged toward the door with a fierce growl. The beam of light disappeared. Max jerked the door open quickly, but saw no one.

"Stay, Sam!" Max commanded. "Stay!" He didn't want Sam to be ambushed. Locking the door once more, he said, "Sam, you scared him away. Good girl! Let's go back to bed."

Unable to sleep, Max lay in bed with his pistol nearby until daylight. His thoughts rambled from his years of work with the agency, to his partner in several very dangerous missions. He'd learned early on to count on Jane, even in the most desperate times. There was a nagging grief on his mind, swirling in and out, of questions about who had killed her and why she was murdered. He finally gave up on sleep and got out of bed. "Sam, stop snoring. How in the hell can you snore so loud?" Sam slept on, undisturbed.

After his ritual coffee, he and Sam began their early morning walk. His face felt numb from the cold air. He was glad he'd worn a heavy jacket. The weather was apt to change on a whim, since it was still hurricane season.

Unexpectedly, a tall stranger with long, flowing white hair jogged up from behind Max. He slowed down to talk. "Good morning," the stranger said. "It's a bit cold, don't you think?"

"Yeah," Max said. Feeling antisocial, he didn't want to get into a conversation with anyone, especially a man he didn't know. To suddenly show up all friendly seemed suspicious.

"Nice dog," the stranger said, making a motion to pet Sam.

Sam growled, her teeth flashing fiercely to confront the man. The stranger jerked his hand away. Max pulled on the dog's leash.

"Pal, I don't think it's a good idea to touch the dog. She's a service dog and trained to protect," Max said.

"No problem. You're smart to have her. You never know what the day is going to bring. It's rough out there. Be careful," the stranger said. "Have a good walk. See you later." He turned around and started jogging in the opposite direction.

Max stopped and looked at Sam. "Girl, what's wrong? Is he a bad man? Is that what you were trying to tell me?" Max squatted down and hugged her. "It's OK." He cut his morning walk short; they returned to the cottage quickly. He didn't want to feel paranoid, but there were too many incidents that didn't add up. He decided to strap his Kimber .380 to his ankle for extra protection when he was out in public.

He picked up the *Eagle Hills Gazette*, and a small article on the fourth page about Jane caught his eye. He read that the coroner had established the cause of death was blunt force trauma. There was a request from the police department, asking the public to provide any information they might have, as the investigation was ongoing. Max knew Jane better than most, but had not been in contact with her in a while. In the old days, they had shared a bed a few times, at first—but as the missions became more intense and dangerous, they chose to forego the sex and focus on their work. He had entrusted her with delicate information again and again, and she always delivered on time. Max had so many questions, but no one to ask. *Did she come to see me? And if so, what for?* He had not been on the radar since the fiasco that nearly got them both killed.

He decided to just let it go, to let it play out, and remain cautious. He spent more than an hour doing an elite military workout that kept him in shape. After the weights, squats, sit-ups, and cardio, he ate his regular power breakfast. He had always been meticulous in taking care of himself. After watching his brother destroy himself with drugs, he'd vowed to never take his health for granted. It had felt good, lying naked with Lily. It wasn't an ego trip; it was simply being able to show her the results of his hard work. He hadn't taken his clothes off for a woman in a good while.

Max thought about his naughty activity with Lily last night. Although it certainly wasn't romantic, it was definitely exciting. It was a first for her—a quickie in a lifeguard shack, of all places. He smiled. He feared he was allowing her to get close to him. Their relationship was beginning to feel like more than just a roll in the hay. That worried him, but not enough to stop seeing her.

He wondered if it was too early to call her, barely resisting the urge. Instead, he got his clubs and left to play a round of golf at the Major Sautter Country Club. He enjoyed playing alone. He could clear his mind, yet at the same time, sort out his problems and make decisions. He felt in charge of his destiny on the green. The warm sun had chased the cold and fog away. It was a perfect day for golf.

Often, he would take Sam with him. The dog would sit regally in the golf cart as her master drove them around chasing a ball. However, this time, Max left Sam at the cottage. He knew Sam would guard their home against any intruder. It bothered him that someone had tried to break in while he was there. He questioned whether it was attempted robbery or a scare tactic. Before he left, he'd mounted a home video camera on the living room wall, hoping to catch anyone if they did get past Sam. With his pistol strapped to his ankle under his pants, Max felt confident as he played on the green.

At the club, he briefly chatted with the golf pro, Vince, who always kept a treat for Sam behind the counter. Max wished he had brought the dog with him. He missed her. She was the only constant in his life.

While Max was chasing balls, Lily and Joanie were hitting the antique shops. The two women spent the entire morning in search of a vintage Singer sewing machine with a foot pedal. It wasn't that either one of them could even sew a button on; it was just that Lily regretted leaving her grand-mother's machine behind in Hoggville.

They were about to give up their search when they went into Angela's Antique Store. Lily enjoyed hanging out in the tiny shop filled with child-hood memories. The owner, Angie, was a delightful young woman who was surprisingly very knowledgeable about every piece of merchandise on the floor. From old thimbles to an antique mandolin and everything in between, she could tell the history and sometimes weave a story.

"Good morning, Lily. Can I help you with anything today?" Angie asked, cheerfully.

"Hello, Angie. I'd like you to meet Joanie. She's visiting me from our hometown," Lily said. "I'm trying to get her to move here."

"Joanie, welcome to our little piece of heaven," Angie said.

Joanie smiled. "Thank you. I would love to just look around, if you don't mind."

"Of course! Take your time," Angie said.

"We're on a mission to find one of those old Singer sewing machines that uses a foot pedal. My granny had one in her bedroom when I was very little. She taught me how to thread the machine, and she let me sew on her scrap material," Lily explained.

"Oh, dear. I did have one, but I sold it last week. I'm so sorry. I'll be on the lookout for another one for you. I still have your number from the time you bought that glass bowl with the gold trim," Angie said. "You see, I remember my customers." She grinned.

By lunchtime, they had run out of places to look but concluded that their mission was not a bust, since Angie had promised to keep Lily in mind. They ended up at the bookstore. Debra was sitting in the back of the store eating lunch. She heard the bell tinkle when the door opened.

"Be right with you," Debra yelled.

"No problem. It's just me. I brought a friend," Lily shouted. "She's from Hoggville."

Debra came to the front of the store moments later. After introductions, she asked, "Lily, where have you been keeping yourself? I haven't seen you in a while. Did you go to the party?"

"Yes, I did. It was very interesting. Lots of people, most I didn't know. I did happen to run into our author, Brock Savage. It was a short conversation because he was quite preoccupied," Lily explained. The vision of Evan the Assassin holding his naked shaft was still fresh in her mind.

"He came in the shop this morning and offered to do another book signing event here. He said he was having a very good time in our little town and had decided to stay longer," Debra said. "I think that's very nice of him, and it sure helps my business."

Joanie picked up Brock's latest book from a table holding a poster picture of him. "Oh my, he's handsome. Now, when is he going to be here?"

"He'll be here tomorrow. There isn't enough time to advertise, but I'm going to put a sign out on the sidewalk. That will be enough to bring in the customers. He's quite appealing," Debra said. "I wouldn't mind a dinner date with him."

"Oh, yeah, Debra, I think you would definitely enjoy his company," Lily said. She almost bit her tongue to keep from telling what she witnessed at the Halloween party.

Lily and Joanie spent the rest of the afternoon back at the cottage, talking about old times and drinking sangria. Lily's special recipe consisted of red wine, orange juice, a generous splash of rum, and thin slices of a lemon, a lime, and an orange. By the time Max called around five, they had cranked up some old '60's music and were dancing in the living room. Lily invited Max over for a drink. He had just finished his round of golf and returned home. He was tired and hungry, but accepted Lily's invitation anyway. He could hear the music in the background when he called her.

Max arrived at Lily's carrying a large pizza and a bag of chips. Joanie was so grateful for food that she offered to pay him. He laughed and told her he would send her a bill. Lily convinced Max to sample the sangria. He liked it so much that he drank three glasses while eating pizza. They were all starved, so not one slice of pizza was left. It was a night to let loose, relax, just enjoy— and that is what they did. They moved the coffee table to the side and the three danced the evening away in the middle of the living room floor. It was fun, another new experience for Lily.

At eleven o'clock, Max told Lily it was time for him to go home. "I've really had a good time with you girls tonight, but I've got to leave. I left Sam alone all day when I went to play golf; I don't want to leave her alone all night too. She's apt to get mad at me. I learned a long time ago that you don't want to make a female mad at you."

The two women laughed, and Lily walked Max outside. "Thank you for coming over. Oh, and thanks for the pizza and chips. You saved us from starvation," Lily said.

"You're welcome." Max looked into her beautiful eyes. He gently kissed her forehead, then her nose, and finally her lips. Lily thought it was incredibly sexy. Just for a moment, he wanted to tell her how he felt. However, reality kicked in when he saw Joanie standing at the window. He released her and left.

When Lily went back inside, Joanie had restored the living room furniture to its usual place, and was cleaning the kitchen. "Girlfriend, he's got the hots for you," Joanie said. "I see how he looks at you."

"Oh, I don't know about that. I mean, he's a good guy, and we really have a great time together. He's taught me so much, I can't even describe it. But I think that's as far as he wants to take it. He backs off quickly. I don't understand it; I'm not chasing him or being at all demanding. Sometimes I feel there is more to him, a past that he keeps hidden. Maybe he'll open up to me in time...or maybe not."

"Be patient, Lily. It will be worth it. It's high time you got some happiness in your life! If he makes you happy, then go for it."

"You're right, as usual. I don't know about going for it, though. I really don't know how. I will just take it day by day and see what happens. 'Que Será, Será.'"

"Yeah, right, Doris Day. Now about tomorrow... Let's go back to the bookstore. I want to take a look at that Brock Savage in person. Hey, I might even buy his book."

Reluctantly, Lily agreed to return to Books4U to appease her friend. Besides, she wanted to check on other books Brock had written. It seemed that she was becoming quite interested in government sanctioned covert operations in foreign countries, even if it was fiction—or so the author said. Remembering her father's stories about his years in the Marines, Lily admitted she'd always been fascinated by military affairs and national security. Besides, she wondered if Brock would remember her from the Halloween party.

"All right, Joanie, we'll go back to the bookstore so you can see Brock Savage. Just don't call him Evan."

It felt like a great ending for a fun night. They laughed and went to bed.

Chapter 10

Not knowing the exact time of the signing, the two women went to the book store after having lunch at Cheryl's the next day. News traveled fast that the author was available again, and by the time Lily and Joanie arrived, there were no less than six of his readers surrounding him. Brock didn't notice Lily and Joanie; he was being interviewed by the local news reporter. Debra motioned to the two women, so they joined her at the counter. Brock was dripping with charm and masculinity, especially when smiling for publicity photos.

To Lily's surprise, Max and Sam entered the shop minutes later. "Hello, ladies. I saw the sign out on the sidewalk and thought I would check out this author. It seems he's very popular, the talk of the town," Max said, looking at Brock's back and long white ponytail.

"It's always good to see you," Lily said. She reached down and hugged Sam.

As Brock Savage turned around, Max recognized the face of the stranger who approached him on the beach. Sam became restless when she saw him. *Something just isn't adding up*, Max thought. *Who is this guy?*

"What's wrong with Sam?" Lily asked.

"Oh, she's probably hungry. I guess I better be going," Max said. "I'll catch you later."

Joanie and Debra said their goodbyes. Max gently squeezed Lily's hand. He glanced back one more time at the author, a man whom Sam definitely did not like. He had learned a long time ago to trust his dog's reactions to people.

Brock didn't notice Max until he was going out the door with Sam. After his brief meeting with Max on the beach, he had hoped he wouldn't run into him after that. *Damn it, I did what I was told to do. If he doesn't take the hint, it's not on me,* Brock thought. *If it isn't contained soon, it's going to get out of hand. She said she would take care of it. Then, she ends up dead. She was one of the best.*

Debra went over to Brock's table to thank him for being so gracious as to give another afternoon to her customers. Although the event only lasted two hours, her business had increased greatly because of the well-known author. Joanie introduced herself to Brock and offered to help him load up his materials and books. Lily remained behind the counter, attempting to avoid any embarrassing exchange.

It didn't work. After Joanie rambled on about visiting her best friend, Brock walked over to the counter. "Hello, Lily. We meet again. But this time, I'm sorry to be out of costume," he said, showing a slight grin.

"Oh, hi Brock. It's good to see you...again," Lily said. *Oh, I saw enough of you to last a long time, big boy,* she thought.

"I hope you've enjoyed your stay here in Eagle Hills," Debra chimed in. "We aren't like a big city, but we have enough talent here to keep us interested."

"I am certainly enjoying the ambiance. My original plan was to stay three days, but I have found it to be just what I needed to get away—and possibly start writing my next book. There's plenty to write about, that's for sure," Brock said.

"Oh, I'll agree on that," Lily said. *Yeah, if I could write a book, it would be a best seller. Plenty of adult content,* she thought.

"It's been nice meeting you, Brock. I've heard so much about you—I mean, about your books," Joanie said.

"Ladies, it's been very nice talking with you, but I am getting hungry. I'm going to try out that seafood place down the road," Brock said. "And Lily, there's no doubt I'll be running into you again." He laughed.

Lily and Joanie stayed at the store after Brock left. They helped Debra close up. Then, all three decided to go over to Ernie's for a quick drink. It was unusually noisy when they entered. There was a crowd around the bar. It appeared that Ernie was performing his favorite bar tricks. Joanie slipped through the crowd and watched. Ernie was too involved to notice her. *He's really good,* Joanie thought. *But I'm better.*

Debra and Lily sat in a booth while Joanie challenged Ernie to a magic coin trick. The crowd roared. Ernie invited her behind the bar and she obliged. She performed the trick to perfection. Ernie was impressed, and so was the crowd.

"Looks like I'm going to have to hire you, Joanie," Ernie said. "That is, if you plan to stay in Eagle Hills for a while."

"Hmm. I'd really never thought about that, until now," Joanie said. "Maybe."

Ernie leaned over and whispered, "I'd like to see more of you."

"I thought you saw all of me the other night," Joanie whispered back.

The three women finished their drinks, tipped Ernie, and left. Debra broke up the trio just outside, bidding her friends good night, and went the opposite direction toward her home. Lily and Joanie walked quickly back to the cottage. There was a cold drizzle pelting their faces, chilling them both to the bone. As soon as they got to the cottage, each one took a quick hot shower to warm up. After drinking hot toddies, they retired to their beds. Both relaxed by reading a Brock Savage book. By ten o'clock, Joanie had fallen asleep with the open book lying to her side. Lily had hoped Max would call, but that wasn't going to happen. His day had been full of surprises.

* * *

After he and Sam left the bookstore, they returned home to see a delivery van leaving. At the front door was a package, wrapped in brown paper and tied with string. There was no return address. He was hesitant to even pick up the package at first, but Sam seemed unconcerned. So Max placed it on the table on the patio, then pulled out his pocketknife and cut the string. He stood over the table, taking his time unfolding the package, still a bit fearful of what it could be. He let out a big sigh of relief when it appeared to just be a bundle of typewritten pages. He was confused. *What in the hell is all this crap? Who sent this? No one is supposed to know where I live.*

Max only noticed his hands were trembling when he sat down. *Damn it!* He gathered the papers and went inside. He hadn't forgotten about Sam's reaction to Brock Savage earlier. There were just so many questions and no answers.

"Sam, I wish you could talk. I know you're trying to tell me something about that Savage guy. I know I need to stay away from him, I just don't know why," Max said. "I thought when I moved out here in the middle of nowhere I could just fade into the background. And we did, ole girl, we did...for a while."

Max gave Sam a bowl of water and a couple treats. "Here you go, Sam. I'm going to look into these papers and find out what is so important about them. You go lay down. Be a good girl."

Max sat down at the kitchen table with the mystery papers to read. Less than five minutes later, he nearly fell out of his chair. *Holy crap! It's about Libya. Wait a minute... I was supposed to be an unknown operative. Intelligence pledged that no one would get ahold of anything from this mission. Damn it! I've had enough. Somebody is going to tell me what is going on. It is bad enough I have to keep a low profile for the rest of my life. I'm not the one who screwed it up.*

After fixing himself a stiff drink, he called the office of Senator John Butcher. Max's vow never to contact Butcher was off the table now. With the ploy of a donation to his upcoming campaign, Max found out from a volunteer that the senator was out of the office, playing golf.

Max left Sam at the cottage and went to the country club. He rode a golf cart around until he found the senator playing alone on the ninth hole. He approached John Butcher as he was choosing his golf club.

"Senator, I need to talk to you," Max said. "It's important."

"I'm sorry, pal, but I don't know you," John said. "Besides, I came out here to get away for a while."

"John. Yes, you *do* know me, and you know why I'm here," Max said. "*Talk* to me."

"No! Get out of here!" John barked harshly. He picked up his club and slung it into the air. "I mean it! Leave, right now."

"Answer me one thing. Is this about me or about Jane?" Max yelled.

John stared coldly into Max's face. "Look, I don't know anything. Don't contact me again." John cursed under his breath, picked up his club, and sped away in his golf cart.

Standing there alone, out in the open, Max suddenly felt too vulnerable. He reached down and felt for his pistol, reassuring himself it was strapped securely to his ankle. He hurried back to the club house, parked the cart, and raced home. It was late afternoon. He opened a bottle of Johnny Walker and drank far too much. He passed out on the couch with Sam sleeping in the recliner.

The morning came too soon for Max, who sported a bad headache and tried to cure his hangover without success. He skipped the morning walk on the beach, letting Sam out just for quick bathroom duty. After their routine breakfast, he read the remaining pages of the transcript. He shook his head. *Have they hung me out to dry? That mess was to be laid to rest years ago,* he thought. *I agreed to cover for him. He was an important target for the rebels, and we couldn't give him up. Damn it.*

Max called Lily just to hear a sane person's voice. He was tired of trying to reason through the recent events. He just wanted some normalcy in his life, and...well, maybe a little loving. He didn't want to drag her into his unpredictable life, but he was drawn to her, even when he wasn't with her.

"I'm glad you called, Max. How is Sam? I was kinda worried about her when she acted all fussy yesterday," Lily said.

"Oh, she's all right. No problem. I was calling to see if you wanted to do something tonight, maybe go see a movie," he said.

"I'll tell you what, Max. Now, don't faint, but would you like to come over here for dinner?" Lily asked. "I know it's a shock, but I really can cook. I just have to go buy food."

"Hey, I'd love to. What time?"

"Make it six. We can have a drink before—and I promise I won't poison you."

"What about Joanie?"

"Oh, she already has plans with Ernie. She called him earlier. He asked her to come to the bar tonight. I get the feeling she'll be staying overnight at his place. Why else would she be using my little overnight bag? Plus, I saw her pack a red nightie she bought at Beverly's."

"OK, Lily, I will see you at six this evening. Can I bring anything?"

"No...maybe some antacid." She laughed. "No, I'm just kidding."

After they hung up, Max felt more at ease. He wanted badly to be in the real, everyday world instead of the one of mystery and intrigue from his past. It was great when he was younger, but the years were catching up with him, whether he liked it or not. It was the simple things he missed. And now with all the confusion of the veiled threat from Brock, the attempted break-in at his home, the package, the strange reaction of the senator, and most of all, Jane's murder, he wondered if he would ever have a quiet life.

Max made a quick run to the liquor store and bought a nice bottle of bourbon. He didn't know what Lily was going to cook, but he knew she drank bourbon. He figured that would fit in with any meal.

Chapter 11

O
h God, I'm going to cook!" Lily found Joanie outside cleaning her bike. It was a sunny day, and Joanie didn't mind the cold. Her bike was her baby. She kept it clean and polished. When Lily told Joanie of her dinner plans, Joanie laughed.

"Honey, are you sure don't want to order a pizza or something? I mean, I've not seen you cook in a long time," Joanie said. "You don't want to make the man sick."

"Oh, good grief. I can cook. I *did* cook. I know I can cook *something*," Lily said. "I'm running to the grocery right now. Do you want to go?"

"Uh, no thanks. I'm finishing up on my baby here, and then I'm going to take a short ride. I won't be gone long. I have to be back in time to shower and clean up to go to Ernie's, at five. I guess you know I may not be back here tonight. Are you OK with that?"

"Sure, no problem. I want you have a good time. Just be careful."

Lily drove to the grocery store because she didn't know what or how much she was going to bring home for their meal. She knew it had to be quick, easy, and taste good. As she pushed her buggy in and out of the aisles, she finally decided on a salad, spaghetti, and garlic bread. She got excited, seeing the wide variety of jarred sauces the store had in stock. *Yeah, this is gonna be easier than I expected,* she thought. She bought premixed salad, a bottle of Parmesan cheese, two jars of sauce, and a box of spaghetti. From the deli, she got a loaf of garlic bread. She was so proud of herself. After checking out, she hurried to her car to load up. Parked beside her was Beverly, loading her trunk with sacks of groceries.

"Hi, Beverly. My goodness, are you stocking up for a long winter?" Lily asked.

"Hey, Lily. No, I locked up the shop to run down here for a few things. I have a dear friend who lost her husband recently, and she has four young kids. She's going through a hard time right now, so I'm kind of helping her. Believe it or not, I know how it feels to do without. What are you doing here? I don't believe I've ever seen you at the grocery store."

"Actually, I asked someone to dinner at the house tonight. I don't really know what got into me, but I'm going to turn the stove on."

"And afterwards, are you going to turn him on? Are you the dessert?"

"Oh no! I forgot to get dessert. What should I do?"

Beverly laughed. "Look, don't worry. I'm going back to the shop to pick up some paperwork. Follow me over there. I have something that is guaranteed to end the evening on a good note."

Lily followed her the short distance to the lingerie boutique. Once inside, Beverly motioned for Lily to come in the back room. To Lily's surprise, she entered a room with walls of shocking pink. Hanging on the walls were various sex toys of different sizes and colors. On a small counter were long pink feathers, pink eye masks, and an array of pink vibrators. She picked up a cellophane-wrapped packet labeled with the word *Edible*.

"Beverly, what in the world is this?"

"*That*, my dear woman, is a pair of edible panties. And if I'm not mistaken, it says they're strawberry flavored."

Lily grinned. "I take it you love the color pink. I swear, Beverly, I've never seen anything like this before. I hardly know what to say."

Beverly laughed. "Don't say anything, my dear. You have entered the wonderful world of sexual gratification. Now, I have something to give you to make your night memorable. Don't worry, it's nothing dramatic; it's just something simple that really turns a man on."

Beverly reached under the counter and laid a pair of pink fuzzy plastic handcuffs on the counter in front of Lily. "Wear these, and he will lose his mind. It's a power thing. I'll show you how to wear them. Don't worry. All you're doing is bringing a toy to your sexual playground."

"Really? Are you sure? I don't know," Lily said. She felt embarrassed.

"Just try it," Beverly urged. "Offer it. I guarantee he'll jump at it. It's all about control. But remember, you can unfasten them at any time. If you don't feel comfortable doing it that way, you can always use the cuffs on him." She showed Lily how to use the cuffs.

Lily took the handcuffs, thanked her, and offered to pay.

"No, it's a gift. Needless to say, I don't advertise this back room. It is only for special friends, so I would appreciate it if you didn't say anything. The church women would have a field day if they knew, the ones who survived their strokes anyway. Actually, they'd probably love to sneak in here. But that's the way it is. If you decide you would like to buy anything later on, just let me know."

Lily left with her little pink bag. When she got home, Joanie was gone with her bike. She put up the groceries and set her little surprise on the bed. She began searching her closet for something to wear for the evening. Lily finally chose deep pink, velveteen slacks with a matching long-sleeved top. She laid out the clothes, including a tiny sheer pink panty and matching bra, on the bed. She figured she would go all pink for the night. Everything would match her handcuffs. She giggled. *Oh, I'm losing my mind here. I feel so naughty! I've never done anything like this in my life. What if he pushes me away? I really want to please him, but I hardly know what I'm doing.* She didn't hear Joanie come in.

"Well, look at *you*, getting all gussied up for your man! Good for you, girlfriend," Joanie teased. "I hope you get lucky tonight. I'm sure going to try."

"*Oh!* You scared me to death! Yeah, I just hope I don't make him sick with my cooking. That would ruin everything," Lily said.

Joanie picked up the tiny pink bag. "What is this?"

"Go ahead and look. I swear, I'm turning into a sex maniac."

Joanie opened the bag and let out a huge cackle of laughter. "Oh, you tramp! And the cuffs are pink too! Is tonight a theme night, and the color is pink? He's going to either think you're nuts or he'll love it. Where did you get it?"

"Well... Don't say a word to anyone, but I got it at Beverly's. She doesn't want everyone to know about it. I'll tell you the whole thing later. Right now, I'd better get in the kitchen and set the table."

"Hey, I'll set the table for you. You concentrate on the cooking. I mean, what are you fixing for the poor man?"

"I've got a great meal planned, I'll have you know. I can't go wrong with spaghetti, right? Just dump two jars of sauce on it. The salad is already cut up. And I got garlic bread, pre-sliced. I'm going to fix him a couple strong drinks before we eat, too."

Joanie set the table for two and then rushed to get ready to leave for Ernie's. Lily began preparing her spaghetti dinner. After Joanie left, Lily hurried to shower and dress. She combed her hair into an up-do and applied more makeup than usual. *Oh god, I hope he doesn't think I look like a Pepto-Bismol doll.* It was too late to change. She placed the handcuffs in the nightstand drawer. *I don't want him to see these right off. If I back out of it, he will never know.*

As usual, Max was right on time. He handed Lily a bottle of good bourbon, apologizing if it wasn't appropriate for the dinner. She assured him that bourbon would complement any meal she prepared. He followed her to the kitchen. It was an easy, friendly moment.

"Something smells awfully good," he said.

"Thank you, Max. I hope you like it." *I hope he likes the dessert later, too. If he doesn't, I'm going to die. Just kill me dead because I will die of embarrassment anyway.*

He noticed her new hairstyle and clothing. *She sure looks good in pink.* "Damn, woman, you look very nice," he said.

Lily poured the drinks and steered him back toward the living room. Neither mentioned the wild sex on that couch the last time they were together. She was determined to make this evening an unforgettable adventure.

"Where's Joanie tonight?" Max asked.

"I ran her off. No, not really. She has a date with Ernie. She said she may stay overnight. I think she's got a crush on our bartender. They have a lot in common," Lily said. "I'm happy for her."

"What makes you happy, Lily?"

The question surprised her. "Well, I don't mind living alone. I was married for a very long time. Every day is a new day for me now. I'm still getting used to doing what I want to do, and taking care of *me*. So, I guess I could say I'm happy right now. My life is in discovery mode. What about you? What makes you happy?"

"Lily, I've been living alone for so long, with the exception of Sam, that I don't know anything different. My wife died more than twenty years ago. We never had any kids. When she passed, I delved into my work; my work became my wife, so to speak. Plus, I have Sam to keep me straight. As far as being happy, I really don't know what happy is anymore. I guess you could say I'm content."

"What kind of work did you do?"

"Oh, I was a jack of all trades. I did a little of this and a lot of that. I made a decent living," Max answered. *I need to be careful; it's getting too personal.*

Lily laughed. "That sure tells me a lot. I guess you will remain my mystery man."

Max fixed his eyes on her face. "I'm not that interesting. I'd rather hear about you."

"Let's just say that I married young, had no children, and I'm now widowed. Oh, and I rarely had the opportunity to travel outside of Tennessee until I moved here," Lily replied. "I'm sure my life is boring compared to yours."

"Not really." He took a swig of bourbon. *Oh, if she only knew.*

Talk settled on common interests: college basketball, trivia, and a love for United States' history. When dinner was ready, they carried their conversation to the table. Lily was pleased that the meal had turned out well. Max showed a respectful appetite.

"Thank you, Lily. This was very good. I haven't had a home-cooked meal in forever." He laid his napkin on the table and pushed his chair slightly back. *The woman can cook.*

"I'm glad you enjoyed it. I don't cook often. I was afraid I had forgotten how. I guess it's like riding a bicycle," Lily said.

They returned to the couch with another round of drinks. She made sure these were stronger.

"You look very nice tonight. Gee, I think I told you that earlier." He inched closer and removed her hair clip, never allowing his eyes to stray away from hers as her thick hair cascaded down around her face and onto her shoulders.

Lily rested her hand on his chest. "Thank you. I wanted tonight to be special."

Then Max took her hand and placed it on the rising mound under his zipper. She gently kneaded his hardness as a soft moan escaped his lips. His heart pounded furiously when she unzipped his pants. She found his naked shaft, grasped it, and slowly rubbed the tip with her thumb. It was more than he could stand; a drop of fluid oozed out. She smiled, enjoying it as much as he did.

She stood up, led him into the bedroom, and gently pushed him onto the bed. After taking his shirt off, she removed her own clothes, keeping on her sexy pink bra and panties. He grinned as she pushed him back, pulling his pants off. He gasped when her lips gently brushed against his manhood.

She dimmed the light, reached into the nightstand drawer, and brought out the handcuffs. Max watched, amused, assuming she would offer them to him. He was surprised when she snapped one of the cuffs onto his left wrist. His desire grew; he trusted her. Raising his arms back, she looped the cuffs around the brass headboard and fastened the other bracelet on his right wrist. She was consumed with a powerful feeling of lust. He watched as she removed her damp panties. Lily was in total control of his body, and she liked knowing he was hers for the taking.

Lying on top of him, she kissed his lips, slipping her tongue in and out of his mouth. He returned the favor. He watched as she slid down, then licked and sucked his nipples. He moaned when she gently nibbled. She moved her body down further, kissing, licking, and softly biting until he trembled. She kissed his inner thighs, teasing his manhood with flicks of her tongue. Her mouth engulfed much of his rod and suckled while in motion, causing Max to gasp. She was prepared to drink his nectar. She saw he was wild in pleasure as he tugged on the handcuffs.

"Lily, baby, please. I can't hold on any longer," he begged.

"What do you want?" she whispered in a voice that was soft and low, with a hint of something Max hadn't heard before. "Tell me."

"Take me inside you now. I need you," he cried.

Lily climbed on top and slid down on his wet, hot pole. She rocked her body in a slow rhythm. Max was helpless; he wanted this feeling to last longer. He desperately fought his release. They looked into each other's eyes, knowing they would peak together. It was fireworks. The sensation was intense. She collapsed on top of him, her body weak and completely spent. She caught her breath, then rolled off him and released the handcuffs.

Lily looked over at the man who had become much more than a friend. *Was that a tear sliding down his cheek? Oh, my God.* She held him in her arms. She watched as he drifted off to sleep. Soon, she joined him in slumber.

Chapter 12

The loud screech of sirens brought both of them out of the bed. Max looked at his watch; it was 4 a.m. Lily grabbed her robe and peeked out the window, yet only darkness prevailed.

"It must be a fire, but I don't see anything close by," she said.

Max wrapped his arms around her. "Hmm...you feel so good. Thank you, baby, for last night. You are full of surprises. Next time we'll change roles. I promise to be good to you."

Lily buried her head on his chest. *Oh, I know you will.*

They were reluctant to let go of each other. While Max dressed, Lily made coffee. She noticed that Joanie's bed was still made. *Thank goodness.*

"Here you go," Lily said, handing Max a cup of black coffee.

He drank half of it. "I've got to go. I don't want you to think badly of me, though. Maybe someday we'll sit down and have a long talk. Please, just trust me for now."

"I do trust you, Max. Whatever it is, don't shut me out."

"If you can't wait for me, I'll understand. If I could tell you more, I would. It's just not a good time...and I don't know when there will be a good time. All I can ask is for you to try to be patient with me. It's very complicated."

Lily nodded and kissed him lightly. "OK. Go on. Call me soon."

"You know I will." He left reluctantly, a smile on his face.

As he got close to his cottage, he saw billowing smoke and flashing red lights. Fearing that it was his home burning, he broke into a run. When he arrived, he saw it was a glowing brush fire. With the wild flames threatening his house, the firefighters set up a control line to suppress and extinguish the blaze. Luckily, there was no wind, not even a breeze to stir and spread embers. The captain of the squad told Max it was definitely arson, as empty gas cans were found at the scene. He asked Max if he had any enemies.

Max denied there was anyone who would want to do him harm. *If I could, buddy, I'd give you a laundry list of those who would be happy to see me dead. Damn it to hell, I just can't keep living like this.* He heard Sam inside the house, barking even louder than the noise of the fire engine. He raced inside, only to be nearly knocked down by the big dog. "It's going to be OK, Sam. I'm sorry." He stroked the dog's back. "I know that smoke upset you." He grabbed the leash and took Sam out of the house quickly, walking down to the beach. He hated it when Sam became scared. He understood very well what fear can do.

The firemen stayed on the scene for another hour before feeling comfortable that the area would not reignite. The captain told Max if he saw any flames, to call 911 immediately. Max thanked each one as they put their equipment back on the truck. He watched as they rolled up the hoses, made one last check around the cottage, and rode away. Inside the house, the odor of burnt growth had dissipated somewhat. Max gave Sam a clean bowl of water and her usual food. Daylight brought the reality closer to Max. If the cottage had burned, he would likely be burying his best friend. Anger rose, cool and analytical, overwhelming his alarm and worry. Revenge was imminent when he was in this state of mind.

Around noon, the firetruck pulled up again. Three firemen flushed the area, wetting it down one more time. Impressed with their dedication, Max told them it took a special breed of person to be a dedicated fireman. They beamed with pride as they drove away.

Obviously, someone was stalking Max. It was becoming too dangerous. He had to take action, stop hanging about in the background. If someone had been sent to dispose of him, why hadn't he been warned? It had happened before, a couple of years ago, and he took care of the assassin in his own way. It was never mentioned again. *That's when Jane helped me disappear. Hey, wait a minute. Oh, crap, was Jane a target because of me? And what about*

71

that Savage guy? What has he got to do with anything? Then there's the senator, who has disavowed any knowledge. Oh hell, that transcript that should not even exist. Too many questions with no answers. I've had enough. I'm going to get to the bottom of this, alone.

He checked in the closet to make sure the PMR-30 was still hidden in the sheets. It had been several days since he'd talked to his friend at the ATF, so Max called him again. He was told that his friend didn't work there any longer. No other information was available. When Max hung up, he felt like he was in a twilight zone. He knew his friend had no plans to retire; the man had been an asset to the agency for decades. *That's it. I will find out why I am being isolated and who is responsible for revealing my whereabouts. I'll make damn sure they pay for this.* Max had learned to deal with his quick temper throughout his military years, but his control was unraveling at a rapid pace. He hated the unknown. *They promised to take care of me.*

He sat at the kitchen table cleaning his Beretta .380. Unsure of what was next, he wanted to be prepared. He hadn't eaten all day. He didn't want to get too comfortable or be distracted. He'd lived that way before...before Samantha. It had been a long time since he felt the walls closing in on him. He trusted his dog more than he trusted himself. Max realized he wasn't alone. He had Sam.

With all the confusion, Max had forgotten to call Lily earlier. When he finally did talk to her, he only mentioned the fire briefly, not wanting to raise a lot of questions. They made a date for the next night to see a movie. He promised popcorn and a coke. The phone call was short because he didn't feel very sociable. "I'll pick you up at about six thirty."

Lily heard a cool, intense tone in her lover's voice when he called. She didn't pursue an explanation for his mood, thinking that giving him some room to decompress and figure out whatever was bothering him was better than twenty questions. The night before had been one of raw lust, and she didn't want to disturb that memory. Exploring a side of sexual desire that she had never been privy to had aroused her naked cravings. The more she gave, the more she craved.

Lily heard Joanie pull up just as she nuked their dinner. Joanie came into the kitchen doing a little dance, with a great big grin on her face.

"Get a plate. I'll share. There's still enough left for the two of us. It's really not bad," Lily said. "How's Ernie?"

Joanie filled her plate and sat down. "We're fine... I mean, he's fine. Lily, I don't know what you're going to think of this, but I want your honest opinion. Not that it'll change my decision, but I want to know what you think."

"OK. You know I will tell you the truth." Lily set her fork down. "I'm listening."

"Ernie has asked me to marry him." Joanie's eyes sparkled. She smiled.

"And? Don't keep me hanging."

"I told him no. Lily, I think I could really love that man. But I can't just load up, move here, and marry a man I just met. I mean, I've already stayed here longer than I planned, partly because of him. But to *live* here...I don't know."

"What have you got back in Tennessee? I mean, really, *think* about it. If you don't want to get married, what's wrong with just moving here? Or, keep your place in Hoggville for security, and stay here most of the time. I just can't see you withering away in that holler. We ain't getting any younger." Lily picked up her fork and shook it at Joanie. "Girlfriend, if he makes you happy, then go for it." *Boy, I'm a fine one to give that kind of advice.*

"He also suggested that I move in with him, and we'd work the bar together, as partners. That surprised me more than the proposal." Joanie took a gulp of her iced tea. "I'm going to think about it. Weigh my options, not let my heart dictate my future. You know I did that once, and it turned out terribly. I am never going to let a man rule my life with fear and intimidation again. You know, it's still unsolved how his sorry ass ended up at the bottom of the Clinch River. I might forgive, but I sure as hell don't forget. You know how I am."

They finished their meal in silence, thinking of the men in their lives. At sunset, they took a short walk on the beach, watching the birds glide with the ocean breeze, appreciating nature and life in general. Wearing jeans and denim jackets, they shuffled barefoot through the sand like children at play. They didn't care when others passed them, staring. They had a bond, from childhood to old age and beyond.

That night, they made a toast and vowed to keep their eyes wide open for any red flags with their new exciting adventures. Although Ernie had been upfront and honest so far about his past, Joanie said she would hold him to the fires of hell if he lied to her. Lily felt frustrated by Max keeping her at arm's length. She wanted to understand why he kept his past in the shadows. The snippets he'd chosen to reveal were not enough. The women stayed up late watching old movies, and sleep came easily for both of them when they turned in.

* * *

It wasn't as pleasant or restful for Max as he lay in his recliner once again, with his loaded gun nearby. He dozed lightly but would jerk awake often in a nervous twitch. His head ached and his body became stiff as the night wore on. He talked to Sam, whose snoring continued to irritate him. By 3 a.m., Max couldn't tolerate the recliner any more. *Damn it, I'm getting too old for this. I'm going to bed.*

"Come on, Sam, let's hit the hay." He motioned for Sam to follow him. "You'll wake me if someone shows up."

The noise of the garbage truck outside his window woke Max around 9 a.m. He skipped his walk on the beach, did a quick workout, and wolfed down his breakfast. His mind focused on who he could contact, who he could trust. With the exception of a couple of times when he was at risk after leaving the agency, he had been successful at staying under the radar. However, due to the uncertainty of the recent events, he figured someone got nervous. Now his life was in peril.

There's one more person who may know what's going on. I haven't seen or talked to Dottie in a long time; I'm not even sure if the contact number I have for her is still active. If she knows anything, she'll tell me. I saved her ass when we were in Libya. She got so mad at me! Gave me a mean right hook, but she kissed me later on. Yeah, I think I'll give her a call. It can't hurt.

It took the better part of an hour for Max to remember Dottie's private phone number. He called and left a message, the standard method to reach her. She returned the call immediately. He told her the facts of the past several days. She listened intently, not attempting to interrupt. When he finished, there was silence.

"Hey, are you still there?"

"Yeah... Max, I think you're in over your head on this. I haven't been privy to what you are telling me, but if you make your presence known, will it help or hurt you? I heard about Jane. I really hate that. She was one of the best agents we ever had. I can guarantee she wasn't in your town for a vacation at the beach. Hey, remember that vacation we had on that deserted beach years ago? The sand dunes nearly swallowed me up when we tried to dig a tunnel." Dottie cleared her throat. "I never thought I'd ever hear from you again. They put you in so deep that I didn't even bother trying to find you," Dottie said.

"I've tried to be so careful. Being antisocial is a snap for me anyway." He laughed. "The agency has always treated me well—until now. Even the senator has distanced himself; that *really* surprised me. He forgot pretty fast, didn't he? Dottie, thanks for talking with me. I was sure if you knew anything, you'd tell me. We go back a long way."

"You know I would. You take care. Just think back, old buddy, of why, and you will find who. It's that simple."

After they hung up, Max thought about their conversation. *Wait a minute. Oh hell. Dottie does know something. She said she didn't know anything about what was going on, but then she said she knew about Jane. And what vacation? We never had a vacation. Hey, she's talking about that mission in Libya. She could have got her cute little ass shot if I hadn't found her. Gaddafi's vast maze of tunnels caused her to panic and those militants were ready for her. OK, this is a start. I hate to revisit all of that misery, all of that death, just to save one man: Senator John Butcher. You son of a bitch!*

Chapter 13

Joanie had spent most of the night wide awake, mulling over Ernie's proposal and moving to Eagle Hills. She'd made her decision by daybreak. She ran into Lily's bedroom and plopped down on her bed, waking Lily with a scare. "Girlfriend, here's what I'm going to do. I'm going to keep my place in Hoggville, like you suggested. I'm going to move in with Ernie and help run the bar. If things work out, then my place in Tennessee will be a vacation home. If not, I can go back home and forget the whole damn thing," Joanie said.

Lily had nearly jumped to the ceiling when Joanie came in. "Oh, you scared me to death! OK, I hear you. Whatever you decide, I've got your back. Of course, you know you can stay with me until you get settled. It's not like I have a whole lot going on in my life...well, except for Max. Even with him, I don't know from one day to the next."

"I'm going over to the bar to discuss it with Ernie. I'll stay here a couple of days longer, then go back to Hoggville. I might even rent my place there for a while. Hey, that's a good idea. I could make some extra money that way."

"OK, go on. I'm glad you're going to move here, even if it ends up being a temporary thing."

Joanie spent the rest of the day at the bar with Ernie. He was elated when she told him of her decision to live with him. While she learned the business of ordering, invoices, and computer programs, Ernie made plans to expand the back of the bar to include another pool table and install a couple of bowling machines. Both were excited by their new adventure.

Lily took the afternoon to clean house and do laundry. Checking the calendar, she was surprised to see that Thanksgiving was getting very close. Back home, she'd always fixed a huge Thanksgiving dinner because Joe invited several of his friends. It was one of the few times in the year that he behaved like a loving husband, since he had an audience. Being desperate for someone to truly love her, she'd pretended to be the happy wife. In truth, she hated it.

Late that afternoon, Joanie came back to a pristine home. An aroma of spices led her into the kitchen, where Lily was at the stove. "Lily, I'm shocked. When did you turn into Susie Homemaker? What smells so good?" Joanie asked.

Lily laughed. "Oh, get over it. It's cold outside, so I made a pot of chili. I mean it's hot, *really* hot, and full of spices. It tastes so good you can hardly stand it. Better get a glass of water ready—or maybe some milk because, did I mention it's hot? Here, try it." She handed Joanie a spoonful.

"Yeah, it's hot, but it's so good! I'm not going out tonight. I've got to make some plans and do some figuring. I told Ernie about my decision, and he was so pleased. I do need to get back home before it gets bad weather. So much to do! I need to winterize my little home, too. You know how awful it gets with the ice and snow. I don't want the pipes to freeze like they did back in ninety-two when we had that blizzard. It got below zero when a transformer blew. Ice formed on the windows, inside the house." Joanie sat down at the kitchen table.

"Hey, I remember that time very well. Our pipes did freeze. Joe went under the house with a blow torch to thaw them out. It's a wonder he didn't set the house on fire."

"Have you got plans for tonight?"

"Yeah, Max and I are going to a movie this evening. I don't know what we're seeing, but I don't really care."

"You're getting serious about him, aren't you?"

"I don't know. Maybe." Lily continued to stir the chili. "I wish I knew him better."

"You do know you're allowed to have a romance, right? I think Max is a good man, and you don't come across many in this day and time. I can see he's really interested in you, too."

Lily gave her friend a small bowl of steaming chili with a large glass of iced tea. "Here, you'll need this to wash it down. It'll make tears come in your eyes."

Max and Sam arrived at Lily's home promptly at 6:30. He asked if Sam could stay there and explained why. Lily understood, saying Sam was welcome any time. Joanie was happy to have a companion for the evening. Sam curled up next to Joanie on the couch as Max and Lily left for the movie.

The theater was within walking distance, like most things in Eagle Hills. Max held her soft hand like they were kids on their first date. It was so obvious he was smitten by this woman who had brought so much excitement into his life. Terrified at times, he was afraid to feel happy. Lily, attempting to keep a level head about their strange relationship, tried to convince herself it was only sex. But she couldn't deny how she felt when he took her into his arms. There was more to their relationship, no matter how hard she tried to deny it; he captured her heart and touched her soul. They were both completely unprepared for their feelings toward each other.

As they stood in line at the ticket booth, Max leaned over and kissed her ear. It tickled, and she laughed. Lily looked up at him, enjoying the way his eyes sparkled. He grinned happily at her every time their eyes met. Once inside, they quickly found seats in the last row, against the wall. He left her briefly to get popcorn and sodas. With just a few movie goers that night, Max and Lily had several empty rows to themselves. The action-packed movie soundtrack echoed loudly, fast cars, explosions, and background music combining into a near-constant roar.

As they sat in the dark, Max turned and kissed her. It was a fierce kiss, his tongue darting in and out. They made out like young lovers often do in a movie theater. His hand slipped under her skirt, moved between her legs, slowly traveled up her thighs, and found her warm nakedness.

"No panties, hmm," he whispered. "What do you want me to do, Lily?"

Lily took a long, slow breath. Earlier, when she got dressed for her date, she'd felt reckless not wearing any panties. She never dreamed she would be sitting in the theater getting a sexual massage. The thought of getting caught faded as he manipulated her womanhood. "Do what you want with me. Now."

He moved his fingers feverishly. As the noise on the screen reverberated, Lily let herself go in an audible moan. It was good. He licked his fingers like she was buttered popcorn. She laid her head on his shoulder for the rest of the movie. She was satisfied; he felt proud.

As they walked back to Lily's cottage, they didn't speak. It was as if they knew their thoughts were of each other. He was hoping she would invite him to spend the night. Sam was already there, so there was nothing to keep him from leaving. Lily wanted him to stay, but she didn't feel comfortable with Joanie in the next bedroom. She was still old fashioned in many ways. She hoped he would take the opportunity to reveal more about himself or what he wanted in life, but neither happened.

After a brief conversation with Joanie and Lily, Max left. Instead of going on the beaten path, he and his dog walked the beach. The wind stirred and a cold rain pelted down for a few minutes. Sam whimpered, pulling on her leash. "Sam, stop that. What's wrong?"

The rain blurred his vision. He wiped his face with his sleeve. A few yards in front of them, he thought he saw a figure of a woman, appearing out of nowhere. He knew her. "Jane, is that you?" he spoke aloud. "Jane!"

Then, the ghost vanished. *What in the hell was that?* Max walked up to the area where the figure had stood. He took out the mini flashlight on his key chain, shining the beam on the sand. "Jane, who's behind all this?" he shouted. "I don't understand."

After seeing that he was alone on the beach, he backed away and continued on home, trying to make sense out of what just happened. He changed his clothes and towel-dried Sam, still lost in thought. *Was Jane's spirit trying to tell me something, or maybe warn me? Did someone keep her away from me? Who had reason enough to kill her? This crap is crazy! Am I losing reality? Wait a minute. Wait just a damn minute. I'll lay odds that she knew I was in danger. She came to Eagle Hills to warn me.*

Max decided to sleep in his bed that night. He couldn't tolerate dozing in the recliner again. He knew that Sam would alert him if necessary. But he kept his gun on the nightstand, just in case. Sam seemed happy to get back on the bed. Despite the episode on the beach, sleep came easily.

* * *

A restful night wasn't so easily found for Lily. She lay awake, staring at the ceiling in her bedroom. She tossed and turned, nearly falling out of bed once. By 6 a.m., she sat in the kitchen, drinking coffee, trying not to wake Joanie. Too many thoughts were racing in her head—too many questions and very few answers. She needed to know where this relationship was heading. *He makes me happy, but happy isn't good enough. Not at our age. I don't know his baggage, but there's no doubt he's got a load. Is all this just a pastime for him, or is it the real thing? What is he hiding from me? Or is he hiding something from himself? I've come a long way, building my confidence since Joe died. I refuse to go back to that place where I felt too timid to speak for myself. I've got to find out where I stand with this man.*

When Joanie came in the kitchen, she said she had moved up her plans. "I'm going back home today, the quicker the better; I need to find someone to look after my place, even if I rent it out, and nobody is going to do that for free. There's just so much on my list, and sitting here thinking about it ain't getting it done. I hope you understand. I called Ernie, and he agreed."

"Oh Joanie, I hate to see you leave, but you're right. You know how fast the weather changes around here. Please, take your time," Lily said.

"I will. I need to leave before the traffic gets too crazy. I'll stop overnight and rest. My bike's in good shape. I'm not worried."

Lily followed Joanie out to her bike and helped her fasten her bag on the rack. They hugged each other, and Lily waved good-bye to her best friend as she rode away. Once inside, she cried, sad to see Joanie leave but happy that her best friend would soon be living in Eagle Hills. *It's all going to work out one way or the other, and for the good. Ernie's good for her. As for me, it's a never-ending story.*

Chapter 14

Lily felt lost without Joanie. She decided she would fill her day by visiting the book store to see Debra, have lunch at Cheryl's, and maybe spend a dollar or two at Beverly's boutique. She'd hoped Max would have called by this time, but maybe she was expecting too much from him. She could never fill in the blanks. *Until he tells me, I can't just assume we are a couple.*

On her stop at Books4U, she found Debra coming out of the back storeroom, somewhat disheveled. "Hey, are you OK?" Lily asked.

"Hi! Oh, I'm fine. I've been shelving and cataloging a new load of books." Debra adjusted her blouse. "I heard the door buzzer. I thought the door was locked." She laughed.

"I just came by to see if you wanted to go to lunch. My friend Joanie is planning to move here. She can be a lot of fun. She's already got a job at the bar, too. She and Ernie have a lot in common. They hit it off immediately. She left this morning, going back home to get packed and have things arranged at her place. She's keeping it, for now."

"Hey, that's great. I'm happy for her—and for you."

Lily looked beyond Debra to see Brock coming out of the storeroom. He was carrying a large stack of books. "Hi, Brock. Always good to see you." *I swear, that man sure does get around.*

"Brock offered to help me rearrange the store. He's been such a big help. Too bad he's going back to New York in a few days," Debra said. "We need someone like him around all the time."

Brock grinned. "Hello, Lily."

"Hello," she replied. "Hey, Debra, I would be happy to help," Lily offered. "I'm getting a bit bored already, with Joanie gone."

"Oh, no, but thanks anyway. Brock and I were almost finished when you came in. I'm not in a big hurry," Debra stated. "By the way, how's that new romance of yours coming along?"

Lily laughed. "I don't know about romance, but Max is definitely quite interesting. I am enjoying his company very much, and his dog, also."

Brock's eyes widened. *Why wasn't I told about this?* "Good for you. You're talking about that man with the dog who was in here at my last book signing, right?"

"Yes. His dog, Sam, was behaving very oddly, so he had to leave," Lily said.

"Have you known him a long time?" Brock asked, trying not to seem like an interrogator, but feeling anxious. Being too inquisitive had always brought him trouble. *Be careful.*

"No, not a long time, but we seem to have a lot of fun together. Why?" Lily asked. *Why do you want to know? It shouldn't concern you.*

"Oh, no reason. I was just making conversation," Brock said. *Damn it.*

"Maybe we all can go out to dinner sometime before Brock leaves," Debra said. "Lily, check with Max and get back to me. Then, we can set a date and time."

Brock set the stack of books down on the counter. He began to check each book into the computer. *That can't happen. I may have to leave Eagle Hills sooner than I planned. I was hoping to stay until instructed otherwise, but it may not be possible. Everything is screwed up and Jane... Poor Jane; I hated what happened. They need to find out who did it. Where was she—or where was she going—when she was murdered? She never got to warn Max. I've tried, but he sure is a stubborn old cuss. I was just trying to scare him with that brush fire. How was I to know that his dog was inside the house?*

"OK, I'll do that. You two get back to work. I'm going to run over to the diner right now. If you finish up soon, come on over and join me," Lily said.

"This job may take a while, but I'll walk out with you," Debra offered.

Lily and Debra walked just past the store and stopped. Lily held back with the questions and let Debra do most of the talking.

"Now, I know what you're thinking—and you're probably right. But just wait a minute. He's the most exciting thing that has happened to me in a long time. In this town, there's not much of a selection of able-bodied virile men. Heck fire, we're used to just checking to see if they have hair and teeth! I know this will never amount to anything, but he really turns me on. He is certainly a man I can get excited over," Debra said. "Do you see what I'm saying?"

Lily smiled and hugged her friend. "I'm the last one to judge. If you're happy, then I am happy for you. I've always got your back. Just don't let your heart ruin it for you."

Debra returned to the store, and Lily went on to Cheryl's diner. Surprised by the crowd, she soon found out that Cheryl had made her special, chicken and dumplings. The recipe had been in her family for decades, all of them always refusing to share it. Cheryl kept her customers on a first come, first served basis. Thus, the filled seats and those waiting in line for her delicious chicken and dumplings resembled a huge family reunion. Lily caught Cheryl's eye and waved to her. Lily pointed outside, to mean she would return later. Cheryl nodded. It was always a very good business day for the diner when Cheryl made her family's specialty.

One last stop—and if Beverly is busy, I'm going back home, she thought. It seemed that everyone had a life that day except her. Usually she was content being alone, but Lily felt restless and was looking for someone to confide in. *I'm getting so involved with Max. Maybe Beverly can tell me what to do. I never dreamed of feeling so much for a man I hardly know. I'm scared.*

Beverly was alone in the boutique. They exchanged pleasantries while having their customary glass of wine. Then, their conversation turned personal.

"Have you used your handcuffs yet?" Beverly asked. "I always want to hear from a satisfied customer." She laughed.

Lily felt the heat rise in her face. "Actually, I have. You were right. It was a fantasy-filled night, for sure."

"Like I said, anytime you need something to make it exciting, you're welcome to go back to the pink room. Glad you enjoyed yourself. I bet your man was happy."

"Well, I think he was very surprised and pleased."

They laughed. Lily told her about the man in her life and the fact that she didn't know much about him. She revealed that her heart was telling her to be patient while her mind was screaming to run. Beverly listened intently, answering with just a word or two. Then, the bomb dropped.

"Beverly, you may know this man. His name is Max. He has a golden lab that's with him most of the time. I'm not sure where he lives, but it's around here close by. He's such a private guy! I don't really know much about him at all."

Beverly nearly dropped her third glass of wine. She muttered, "No, I don't believe we've met. Tell me again, how long have you been seeing him?"

While Lily repeated her story, Beverly's thoughts whirled in a panic. *That low-life piece of nothing! He should have been taken out a long time ago. If Jane had minded her own business, she would still be alive. At least Max has kept his mouth shut about his connections with my brother.*

Lily wasn't aware that she was putting herself in harm's way. In her small world, she assumed all were truthful and innocent. The wine washed away her shyness. However, she was seeking answers from the wrong person.

"Honey, I don't know what to tell you about matters of the heart. Just be patient," Beverly said. "It'll work out." She choked on her words.

"You're right. I'm sorry I bothered you all day with my stories."

There was an uneasy moment between the two women as they emptied the bottle of wine. While Lily thought of her night with the pink handcuffs, Beverly's mind stirred up the terrible drama she wanted to forget. After Lily left, Beverly locked up the shop, turned off the lights, and sat in the darkness. She relived that dreadful night and the violence.

Jane's Visit

Beverly wasn't expecting any visitors that evening. She was surprised when Jane knocked on her door. After Jane explained that she knew the senator's relationship to Beverly and had assisted the senator in finding her, Beverly invited the woman inside.

Jane unintentionally heard of the senator's attempts to find his sister through various adoption agencies. The firstborn, Beverly, was adopted by a couple who died later in a car crash. She was in and out of foster homes, and ended up living on the street most of her life. John, separated from his sister at an early age and placed in the foster care system, was never told of his sibling until he found a distant cousin who accidently let it slip at their first meeting. With a lot of sleuthing, she found Beverly in a California homeless shelter. John brought her to Eagle Hills, coached her, and provided for her monetarily. He tried to make up for all her hardships, sometimes providing to excess. To protect his sister from the media and to shield his political ambitions, they had decided not to expose their family laundry.

Once inside, Jane slipped her shoes off at the door and followed Beverly into the living room. Jane didn't waste any time. "Beverly, I know you love your brother. I'm asking you to help me keep him from making a bad mistake. I'm sure you know John's reelection is very important to him. His political career is everything to him. Unfortunately, he's making a desperate attempt to hide the incident in Libya by eliminating who he thinks is a threat. I have proof that he is trying to remove Max Trainor. He led the outfit who rescued John from the rebels. This just can't happen."

"Oh my God. I don't understand; what do you mean? I don't know anything about John's business. The only time he spills the beans is when he's drunk. One time he did talk to me about being held hostage in Libya, but I thought he was lying. There have been rumors that he's ruthless, but I've never seen that. That's not the man I know."

"I'm asking you to talk to the senator. It's because of John that Max no longer works for the agency. He's saved countless lives, including your brother's."

"Look, I can't change his mind in whatever he does. I want no part of this." Beverly's voice quivered. She abruptly stood up, gesturing for Jane to leave.

"OK, let me put it to you this way. I'm going to tell Max everything I know, including the fact that the man he saved is trying to kill him. Then, we'll see what happens. I'll not sit back and see a good man murdered," Jane said, angrily.

Beverly panicked. In a fury, she grabbed a heavy crystal ashtray, stepped back to the edge of the couch, and hit Jane in the back of her head with all her strength. Jane jerked forward, slumping down onto the floor. Beverly screamed. She threw the ashtray against the wall. "You're not going to ruin my brother's life or mine. Now get up! Get out of here! Don't come back!"

No answer. Beverly bent over and shook Jane's shoulder. The woman's eyes were fixed, her body lifeless. "Oh, God! *No!*" Beverly felt for a pulse. Nothing. She shook Jane's shoulders. "Get up, Jane!" *I've got to call John. Oh, what a mess I have made now.*

Beverly's hands shook as she called her brother. After a series of incoherent ramblings on the phone, John finally understood what had happened. "Will you just shut up? Don't call the police! I'm on my way," John said. Within fifteen minutes, he was at her door. "Good Lord, Beverly, what in the hell have you done?"

Beverly dropped to her knees and burst into tears. "I'm so sorry. I got scared, and I panicked. She said you were going to kill a man named Max, and she was going to ruin you. I know you're not like that, and I couldn't let her hurt you—so I hit her. I didn't mean to kill her. I just wanted her to stop. Don't be mad at me. I didn't know what else to do."

"OK, OK, what's done we can't take back. Go get a quilt. Let's wrap her up and carry her to my car. We've got to get rid of her. Where's her car?"

"She must have walked up here."

"Good. We'll drop her at the beach. Hurry up!"

It was a struggle for them to carry the body to John's car and stuff her in the trunk. The beach was empty when they rolled Jane's body out on the sand. They didn't speak until they were back in the car, returning to Beverly's house

"Why wasn't Jane wearing any shoes?" John asked as they pulled into Beverly's driveway.

"Oh, no! She took them off at my door," Beverly replied.

John's breathing sounded labored. He was exhausted. "OK. When you go in, you put those shoes in the garbage. Then, you use bleach and scrub everything, *especially* that ashtray. Look on the couch and carpet for blood spots. If it takes you all night, that's just too bad. Now, I am warning you, my dear sister, you do not say a word to anyone. You keep your mouth shut if you don't want to spend the rest of your life in prison. Do you understand?"

Beverly nodded. "Yes."

When Beverly was safely back inside her house, John drove away.

* * *

Since that manic episode, Beverly couldn't escape the nightmare vision of Jane's lifeless body crumpled on the floor, seeing her blood-soaked hair and remembering the feeling of tossing the body on the beach like a bag of trash.

Chapter 15

When Lily arrived home, she received a call from Angela's Antiques. "Hi, Angie. Have you got something good for me yet?" Lily asked.

"I sure do. If you can drop by, at your convenience of course, I can show you a vintage Singer sewing machine that just came in," Angie said. "I think you'll be pleased."

"Hey! I'm thrilled already. Listen, just go ahead and put a "Sold" sign on it. I'll come by and pick it up in a couple of days."

"Don't you want to know the price, honey?" Angie asked.

"I don't care. I want that Singer more than anything. Thank you so much for calling me. I'm so excited!"

Lily spent the rest of the evening in her recliner, watching television, waiting for Joanie to call. *The whole day would have been a bust if Angie hadn't called. I can't wait to get that Singer! I may not be able to sew a button on, but it brings back so many good memories.*

Later that night, Joanie finally called. "I've about frozen my ass off, it's so damn cold. I've stopped at a dinky motel near the state line for the night. There's a hole in the wall restaurant across the street, so I'm going to get a hot meal."

"I'm sure glad you called. I was getting a little worried about you. How's the traffic?" Lily asked.

"It's not bumper to bumper traffic because I'm taking the country roads. You know, I could have ridden on home in a couple of hours, but my hands and face are numb."

"No, you're doing the right thing. Take your time. For sure, you don't want to get sick from the trip. I'm so happy that you are coming back here to live! We'll have such a good time."

"Yeah, me too. I think I made the right decision. I'll call you in a day or so and let you know what's going on."

They said their good-byes, and Lily settled back into her recliner, thinking of the conversation with Beverly earlier. *I don't know if I was imagining it, but Beverly sure did act kind of odd after I told her about Max. She was fine before that; then, she seemed to get preoccupied. I hope I didn't say anything wrong. The look on her face was just so serious.*

Lily picked up one of Brock Savage's books and made an effort to delve into the imagination of an author with whom she had become very familiar lately.

* * *

Over at the Trainor cottage, Max closed his eyes for a nap. Being unable to rest caused him to be on edge. He didn't want to have an episode, so he decided to take advantage of a couple of hours of peace and quiet. Unfortunately, it didn't last. He was jolted awake by a loud knocking on his front door. With Sam at his side and his gun in hand, he yanked the door open.

"Damn it, Max, get that gun out of my face!" Dixie yelled.

Standing there in his briefs, Max quickly lowered the gun. "Dixie, what in the hell are you doing here? I could have shot you." He reached out and hugged her.

"Are you going to invite me in or what?" she asked. "It's cold out here."

"Come on in. I'll fix you a cup of coffee, if you want."

"Yeah. I'll take one." Dixie sat down on the couch. "Go put some pants on, too. I don't want to look at your ugly legs."

"Dixie Doodle, you know you love my legs," Max teased, then went to the bedroom and put on a pair of jeans.

"You know you're the only one allowed to call me that, Charlie Horse."

Dixie had been Max's partner in the early part of his career. Together, they had successfully completed some complicated and dangerous missions. They worked well together, maybe too well. The agency had separated them against their wishes after the Libya mission. Max knew it was serious when she showed up.

Max introduced Dixie to Sam, but the animal completely ignored Dixie's attempt to make friends. "Sam doesn't like me," Dixie said. "I'm usually pretty good with dogs."

"I think it might be a female thing," Max said. He winked.

Sam nudged Dixie to scoot over on the couch. Dixie obliged. Then, Sam stretched out next to her.

"Now look at that, Sam does like you," Max said.

After a few minutes of catching up, Max couldn't wait any longer. "Look, Dixie, I don't know why you're here, but it must be important. Talk to me. You know how impatient I am."

Dixie set her cup down on the end table. "There's a lot going on that I have accidently, on purpose come across. It seems to all circle back to that mission in Libya."

Max spewed coffee back in his cup, nearly choking.

Dixie laughed. "Yeah, I know I'm not privy to all the info—but hey, I'm good at what I do. You know that."

Max stood up. "I thought it was a dead issue. That's the whole damn reason I agreed to retire!"

"Sit back down. It's going to be a long night. I can see that now. I'm going to tell you what I know. Then, I'm going to tell you what you need to do. So, just shut up and settle down."

An air of tension filled the room as Max paced, visibly upset. Finally, he sat back down. "OK, I'm listening."

"No one sent me here; I'm on my own. You know John Butcher is up for reelection. Somehow, there's been a leak at the agency, and his fake stories are compromised. The agency tried very hard to keep it contained, but somewhere, there's a lot of money floating around. It seems a few people think you are expendable, in order to keep that coveted senate seat for Butcher. The government does not want the media to get ahold of the details about rescuing that greedy crook. Only the Intelligence Committee knows about the rebels kidnapping the senator, with the exception of a few others. It saved the White House from embarrassment that one of our senators is guilty of bribery in a private oil deal. When the mission didn't go as planned and three were killed, the agency determined that everyone involved would plead ignorance. I have reason to believe your life is in danger."

Max cursed, waking Sam.

"Settle down. There's more, and you aren't going to like this, either. I have reason to believe that Jane was murdered to keep her away from you. She worked with Butcher's office; tons of information fell into her lap on a daily basis. Also, I'm aware of your call to the ATF regarding the gun you found in front of your house. It seems that the guy you asked to do research for you is no longer available. In fact, he's disappeared. Obviously, the owner of that gun deserves protection for some reason. I confess that I'm the one who sent you the package. I thought you would take the hint that there's a target on your back. Oh, and for heaven sakes, don't get all bent out of shape about Brock Savage. He's one of us. We have been on you twenty-four seven, but it's getting to be too much. You're going to have to make some decisions."

"You know, I'm getting really pissed, I mean *really pissed*. Just how closely have I been monitored?" Max asked.

Dixie laughed. "Honey, you need to get that green, fungus-covered bowl of pasta out of your refrigerator."

"That's *it*. Damn it to hell. Just tell me who killed Jane." Max's face turned beet red.

"Honestly, I have my suspicions, but I have no proof. I believe the killer or killers are not agents. I just don't know at this time."

"So, what now? What's next?" Max asked.

"It's up to you. Deep down, you know the protocol. I don't want anything to happen to you. We go back a long way."

Max grinned. "Yeah, we did have some good times, didn't we?"

"There's another issue I need to address, old buddy. I see you enjoying some female company, a woman named Lily—from Kentucky, I believe."

"She's from Tennessee. Why?"

"You *know* why, Max. I'm sorry. You deserve to be happy, but it is what it is."

Another string of curse words spilled from Max. "For God's sake, Dixie, you've really put me under a microscope."

"Damn it, I said I was sorry. I don't like this crap either, but I care about you. I'm laying the facts out. It's up to you."

They stared in silence, reading each other's mind. Dixie knew more than she was telling Max. Holding back some confirmed information about Jane's death protected Max from making a huge error in judgement. Knowing him so well, she figured all hell would break loose if she told him; his temper boiled on the brink of eruption.

Dixie got up to leave. "I'm really sorry, old buddy. You know I've got your back. The agency took care of Jane's burial; she's in the federal cemetery. There was no funeral service, just a private burial. If I find out anything else, I'll let you know. Be careful. I'll be around if you need me. I owe you."

Max hugged her. "Don't worry. I'm going to take care of this. Thank you."

After Dixie left, Max unraveled. *I don't understand why that no-good, sorry excuse for a man thought I was going to interfere in his reelection. I don't give a damn about him. I just did my job. I'm going to call on the senator very soon and sit down for a nice chat, whether he wants to or not.*

It was a long night for Max. He thought about the covert mission and the three on his team who didn't make it back. Still awake at daylight, he was exhausted.

Mid-morning, Lily's phone rang. "I'm really not up to going out tonight, but I would like to come over for a while. That is, if it's all right with you," Max said. "I just want to talk."

"That's fine with me. The weather's supposed to turn bad later anyway. How about coming over around seven?" Lily sensed an urgency in his voice.

After they hung up, Max called an answering service and left a series of numbers that only his contact could decipher. He knew it was time to disappear soon...once again. *Damn it, I don't want to leave! She won't understand... I've got to keep her safe. I love that woman. I thought this last move was permanent. Damn it to hell.*

He had no time frame as to when he'd vanish, but he would be ready. He didn't know his destination yet, but it really didn't matter. He was confident that arrangements for his next home were in progress. Almost immediately, his contact returned his call, confirming the move was set for tonight. He packed his battered suitcase and stashed it in the truck. Eventually, his whirlwind thoughts converged on one subject: Senator John Butcher. *I'm not leaving until I confront that son of a bitch.* Max took the mystery gun out of the pillowcase and put it in his glove compartment. *Let's just see if he knows anything about this gun.*

By six o'clock, with Sam in the back seat, Max drove past the senator's office. He noticed a light shining through the office window, although it had closed over an hour earlier. He was surprised to see the senator's car parked in front. *Well, this is just too easy.*

Max called Lily to say he might be a little late. She didn't mind. He parked his truck on the side of the building. He put Sam on a leash and tucked the .22 into the back of his belt. He went around to the rear of the office and quietly flipped the lock on the door.

Hearing a shuffling noise, the senator looked up, shocked to be facing the man he wanted dead. "How in the hell did you get in here? Get out right now, or I'm calling the police," John yelled. "You're breaking and entering, Max. I'll put you in jail!"

Max took a seat in front of the desk. Sam lay down next to the chair. "Now, John, if you really want to call the cops, then go right ahead. I have nothing to hide. Do you? I believe we've got some things to discuss. To begin with, just so you know, I don't give a damn about your political career. I don't give a damn about you. I was only doing my job, saving your fat ass. I have no agenda to ruin you. You will hang yourself soon enough, you crooked son of a bitch."

Beads of sweat dripped down John's face. His hand shook as he set his cigar in the ashtray. "You wait just a damn minute here. Who do you think you are?"

Max reached behind his back, pulled out the gun, and placed it on the edge of the desk. "I guess you don't know anything about this, either."

John's eyes widened, and he gasped. He reached for the gun, but Max was quicker. "Oh, no, Senator, you're not getting this. It's yours, isn't it? It's a nice pistol, silencer and all. You left it somewhere in a hurry one night, and you were too chicken to come back for it. Must have worried you some."

"Look, let's see if we can work this out. Give me the gun and walk out of here. Nothing will be said. I guarantee the agency will take good care of you," John said. "Deal?"

"Surely you jest. I don't need anything you're offering. Oh, and by the way, I'm keeping this gun; I'll make it a very important part of my collection. Let's just say it's for my health insurance. I look forward to seeing your mug splashed all over the news, but I'm not the one who wants your dirty laundry waving in the breeze. I think there's more than the illegal oil deal you want to keep hidden, too. You've screwed up once again, haven't you?" Max laughed. "I think you'll look good in prison orange."

Max got up and started toward the door, Sam at his side. John stood up, grabbed a letter opener, and lunged at Max. Sam made a dive for the senator's arm and clamped onto it, ready to shred the man. Max ordered Sam to stand down; he didn't want her to get hurt. John knew he was about to lose everything and fought desperately to get the gun out of Max's hand. During the struggle, the pistol discharged; the bullet hit the senator in his foot.

John Butcher slumped to the floor, bleeding. "I'll get you, Trainor! One way or another, I'll get you. I know about your sweet little woman, too."

"Damn it to hell! Let's see how you get out of this one, Senator Butcher." Max motioned Sam to the back door. They left the senator cursing as he crawled to his desk to get his phone.

After Sam leapt into the truck, Max placed the gun under his seat. He straightened his rumbled clothes, checked for any bloody splatter, and combed his hair. He needed to at least be presentable before they got to Lily's.

He wasn't very late, but he apologized anyway. Lily turned the TV to Animal Planet for the dog while Max made himself a stiff drink in the kitchen. He didn't waste any time, gulping it down. He made himself another, and one for Lily. She noticed that he was on edge.

"Max, are you OK?" she asked. "Would you like me to fix you a sandwich or something?"

He took her in his arms, kissed her softly, and buried his head against her breast. "No, Lily, I've got a lot on my mind right now."

At that moment, he looked into the eyes of the woman he wanted desperately to be his. He felt a superhuman desire to make love to her, to give his entire being to her. He picked her up and carried her to the bedroom. He was consumed with the desire to please her, to satisfy her, to fulfill her fantasies. She was all he wanted.

Lily lay back as he undressed her. Silent, savoring his tender touch, his gentle hands on her body, and the sweet kisses on her breasts, she surrendered. She was aroused by the flick of his tongue in the folds of her womanhood. She clenched her hands on the bedsheet, holding in her rising desire. He knew her body. His hard shaft ached, yearning to be inside the woman he loved, but he kept his pace, giving her the freedom of enjoyment.

"I want to make love to you," he whispered.

"Yes," she uttered. She had longed to hear those words from him.

Lily watched him remove his clothes and lay down beside her. His naked body caused her to tremble with excitement. Stroking her thighs, he spread her legs. He moved on top of her, gently kissing her soft belly. He loved her taste as he deftly explored her love nest. Her scent was bewitching. She quivered. It was a passion of a different kind; it was love. His throbbing, rock-hard member craved to be satisfied. He mounted her, sliding in slowly, feeling her hot wetness. She moaned, and he grasped her hands to hold on as he rocked with intense rhythm. She was his.

Consumed with an unbridled lust, she clawed at his muscular back. As the tempo increased in fervor, he drove deeper into her womanhood. Unable to hold back, they reached the summit and became one. As Lily's breathing eased, her eyes filled with tears. She felt beautiful. He held her in his arms for a long time. Not a word was spoken; there was no need, not then.

After their moment had subsided, he knew he couldn't avoid the pain he was about to inflict. "Lily, we've got to talk. Well, I mean, I haven't told you much about myself. I can't put it off any longer."

They dressed and sat on the edge of the bed.

"I've been waiting. You know I'll listen."

He couldn't look at her; he stared down at the floor. "I just hope you understand that there are some things I cannot tell you, or anyone. I ask you to trust in me."

For the next half hour, Max told Lily about his work, careful not to reveal sensitive details about the agency or his missions. He explained that due to the dangers from his last assignment, it had been necessary for him to retire. He added that until notified otherwise, he would never have the comfort of living in a permanent place.

"Are you saying that you are...in witness protection, or undercover? If you're retired, why is there danger?" Lily asked.

"Honey, it's very complicated and involves some government officials. I do not have a life of my own. Those I associate with could be in danger, too. I can't take the chance of placing you in jeopardy."

"What exactly are you saying, Max?"

"I have to leave. Tonight. Now."

"When will you be back? When will I see you?" NO, *this can't be happening.*

Max looked away, then shook his head. "I don't know." *I can't stand to hurt her like this. It's not right. She's innocent in this mess. I have to protect her.*

Lily couldn't think of anything to say. She wanted to scream, to beg him to stay. She said nothing—until Max stood up to go.

"Wait a minute. Can't you stay a little longer? Can't we work this out somehow? We can't end like this." She burst into tears.

Max hugged her. "I'm so sorry. I wouldn't hurt you for the world. Please forgive me." He held her hand as they went into the living room.

Lily stood there, helpless, watching Max open the front door. Her mind screamed for him to stay. As if captured in a slow motion, he turned and held her tear-stained face in his strong hands. Her sad blue eyes engulfed his emotions as he felt her pain. He kissed her forehead. The silence was deafening. An entire encyclopedia of feelings invaded his thoughts. He released her and walked toward his vehicle as she whispered, "I love you." His heart was pounding so loudly he didn't hear her. He needed to focus. His body trembled as he struggled with his desire to run back to her. Forcing himself to get into his truck, he wished he'd never met her. Life was easier before that day at the beach. He quickly wiped a tear from his cheek.

She couldn't shut the door...not yet. In her desperation to prolong the inevitable, she hoped he would get out, race to her, and profess his love. But she knew he was a realist, a man of strength and integrity. She understood why he was leaving; she just didn't want to accept it.

Max sat in his truck, staring at the dashboard. The golden Labrador retriever settled in the back seat. Sam's soft whimpers seemed to say she understood her master's pain. "It'll be OK, Sam." he said, reaching back to reassure his companion.

Finally, Max turned the ignition key and backed out of the carport. He glanced over to see Lily, the woman he had come to love the last few months, still leaning in the doorway. Broken and confused, nothing had prepared him at this late stage in life to meet a woman who made him feel so alive. Her smile, her laugh, and her desire to enjoy the moment caused him to forget his past and grasp for a chance to linger in her world. Yet, reality crept in like an unforgiving, evil force. He had to leave; he had no choice. *Wait for me, Lily. I love you. I'll hold you in my arms again soon. I promise.*

As she gave a feeble wave, Lily watched the man she loved drive away from her home, away from her life, and away from her. The tears flowed, unchecked. She closed the door, locking it as if to keep out all the hurt. She would wait. She knew it wasn't over. *I love you,* she thought.

Chapter 16

Weeks had passed since Lily watched Max slip out of her life, away from her arms. It was difficult accepting his explanation; however, this was not because it was unreasonable. Frustration took hold of her thoughts. *He could have at least called by now. He drifted into my life like a warm breeze on a cool autumn night, and then he just left. Before he came, I felt quite content being alone. Hell, I lived alone in my heart the whole time I was married to Joe. But when I was with Max, a whole new world opened up right in front of me. Damn him!*

Joanie returned to Eagle Hills just in time for the holidays. Spending Thanksgiving with Joanie and Ernie at the bar created a perfect diversion. Lily didn't have time to think about the man who disrupted her life, the man she sometimes wished she'd never met. Ernie provided a huge turkey dinner with all the trimmings, delivered to the bar from Cheryl's Diner. While Cheryl fed the homeless at her restaurant, Ernie fed those at the bar. Christmas proved a nice repeat for friends, family, and anyone who entered Ernie's Nest. Joanie's idea for a group tree decorating delighted everyone on Christmas Eve. With holiday music in the background, a large tree covered with twinkling lights and decorations brought Joanie and Lily a happy sense of belonging. After Ernie placed the star on the top of the tree, he grabbed Joanie and twirled her around, kissing her as everyone applauded. On Christmas Day, Lily and Joanie dressed as elves to give out presents to those with small children. Ernie's Nest was filled with joy.

Although Lily felt pleased that Joanie found love with a good man, thoughts of her life back in Tennessee brought a brief pang. Lily had become accustomed to Joe's absence most holidays, knowing that he spent his free time with his latest lover.

On New Year's Eve, Lily Roberts lost herself in the flames of a bonfire on the beach. Even though Joanie sat on the quilt next to her, she felt lonely. The holidays were winding down. She wanted to look forward to a new year—and maybe, a new self.

"Lily, look! It's wonderful! Ohh! I've never seen fireworks like this in my life," Joanie said, pointing to a falling shower of red, white, and blue sparkles. She applauded while giving a standing ovation.

"Yeah, I don't ever remember seeing anything like this back home. I'm so glad that you moved here. We've been best friends forever. Hoggville, Tennessee will never be the same without the two of us. I wonder who will be the gossip topic of the week now," Lily mused.

"I never thought I would get out of that hard scrabble-existence, much less move away. Thanks to you, I have a good job and a good man. Those old biddies in the holler will just have to spread their lies about each other now." Joanie laughed. "By the way, Ernie said he wants us to come to the bar after the fireworks. Is that OK with you?"

"Sure. I don't have anything else to do," Lily said. "Besides, we have to bring in the New Year with a toast. You have no idea how grateful I am to enjoy the holidays with you and Ernie. You know how hard the holidays are for me. Thank you."

"You don't have to thank me, or Ernie, for that matter. I told him you're the sister I never had," Joanie said.

By the time the bonfire died down to embers and the fireworks ceased, it was getting close to midnight. Lily folded the quilts while Joanie collected the empty beer cans. The beach was nearly deserted as the two women walked the short distance to the bar. Having a vast experience in bartending, Joanie took over the bar during the day while Ernie tended to the patrons in the evening. Although they had much in common, Joanie refused to consider marriage to Ernie, even though he'd hinted several times. When she left Hoggville, there were still questions swirling around about her last husband's body floating in the Clinch River. Of course, no one in town would have blamed her. Hospital records showed she was treated repeatedly through the years: a broken nose, several fractured ribs, and a deep puncture wound. Marriage had left a foul taste in Joanie's mouth.

There were sounds of laughter and music emanating from inside when Lily and Joanie arrived at Ernie's. Lily leaned over to Joanie. "Look who's sitting at the bar. I swear, I believe it's Brock Savage. What in the world is he doing here, instead of bringing in the New Year on Times Square? You know, he gave me the creeps when he had those book signings at Books4U. He boasts of being a conspiracy theorist. I think Debra asked him to help her rearrange the shelves in her store, but somehow I think he rearranged her also." Lily giggled. "Remember when I told you that I interrupted him and Beverly in a closet at her party? He does get around."

"It's really getting crowded in here. I'm going to have to help Ernie behind the bar." Joanie nudged her girlfriend. "Look! There's an empty stool right beside Brock. Go on and get it, quick! Otherwise, you'll be standing against the wall the rest of the night."

As much as Lily didn't want to strike up a conversation with a man she'd seen dressed up as Evan the Assassin, with his massive shaft hanging out, she grabbed the stool. *I wish I could get that vision out of my mind.*

Lily figured she might as well break the ice and play nice. After all, it was the last day of the year. What could happen?

Lily tapped Brock on his arm. "Well, Brock Savage. I'm surprised to see you back here in this little town on New Year's Eve. Aren't you going to miss all the excitement in Times Square?"

Brock turned away from the television mounted on the wall. He smiled. "It's always good to see you, Lily. Have you been enjoying the holidays?"

"Yes, but I'll be glad to bring in a new year. Will you be having another book signing at Debra's bookstore?"

"No, I'm just taking a few days to unwind and write. I'm staying at the inn, like the last time I was here. Beverly invited me to stay at her house, but I graciously declined. I'm set in my ways and enjoy being alone. How about you? Have you made any resolutions?"

"No, and I don't plan to; I end up breaking every one of them."

"Can I buy you a drink? You know you can't sit here with all these drunks and stay sober." Brock laughed.

"Sure. Thank you." *Quit looking at his crotch. Get that scene out of your mind.*

Brock ordered a rum and Diet Coke for Lily and another scotch for himself.

"How did you know what I drink?" Lily asked.

Although very busy behind the bar, Joanie kept her eye on Brock. Lily glanced over to Joanie at one point and winked. Joanie nodded and smiled.

As the ball began to drop, everyone stood up in front of the television and started counting. Streamers sailed through the air while party horns blew. When the New Year arrived, everyone in the bar cheered, toasted, and kissed their neighbor.

Standing beside her, Brock turned to Lily. Slipping his arm around her waist, he drew her to his chest. "You don't mind, do you?"

Lily was taken off guard. She felt frozen against his hard body, mesmerized by his haunting eyes. "Uh, OK."

In the midst of a crowded room, Brock bent down and softly kissed her lips. Lily didn't want to respond, but her body didn't ask her mind. He felt it and kissed her again, this time with the tip of his tongue exploring the inside of her mouth. He pressed his hardness against her. It was too much for Lily; she quickly pulled away.

"Happy New Year, Brock!" She tried to make light of what just happened. She wanted to leave, but she couldn't, not right then. *I'm going to have a major hot flash right now if I don't excuse myself. Damn, he's good.*

"Hey, are you leaving me already?" Brock's sheepish grin irritated Lily.

"I've got to find Joanie so we can make a toast. I promised her. I'll catch you before I leave. Glad you're enjoying your time in Eagle Hills."

Lily disappeared among the patrons, finding Joanie and Ernie in the storeroom. Instead of sneaking in a quickie to start the year off right, the couple was loading up fifths of liquor to restock the bar. Business was booming that night.

Joanie giggled. "Hey, you don't have to give me any excuse. I was standing two feet from you when the ball dropped. I've been ignored before. Brock really turned on the charm, didn't he?"

"I'm sorry I missed our toast. Don't give me grief about that man. He took me by surprise. You know he's just a one-night stand type. I don't need that," Lily said. "Is there anything I can help you with back here? I want to avoid Mr. Savage as long as possible."

"Great. If you don't mind, it would a big help if you restocked the shelves with the opened cases of liquor. That would save us some time before I have to close up," Ernie said.

"Sure. When I'm finished, a toast is in order," Lily said.

Joanie and Ernie returned to the bar. The noise of the party grew louder, even filtering into the store room. Lily concentrated on the labeling, arranging bottles on the shelves for easy access. She didn't hear him come in.

Brock laid his hand on her shoulder. "Can I help you?" he asked.

Lily jerked forward, nearly dropping a fifth of scotch on the floor. "Damn you, Brock Savage! You scared the hell out of me. What are you doing back here?"

Brock snickered. "Well, I got worried about you. I hoped you would come back to my room at the inn for a drink later tonight." His lips grazed her skin as he whispered in her ear.

"Look, I appreciate your invitation, but I must decline. Besides, Beverly is my friend, and if I'm right, Debra is on your list, too. I'm not planning to be on any list. I don't share."

He ran his hands over his long flowing hair. He laughed. "OK, I can wait. You'll change your mind. That man of yours isn't coming back."

"What do you mean?"

"You'll find out soon enough. If you're as smart as I think you are, you'll mark him down as a lost cause. I'll bet he's forgotten about you by now."

Brock returned to the bar, leaving Lily standing there speechless. She fought back the tears as her anger rose to the surface. *How does he know so much about me and Max? It's none of his business. Wow, what an ego! I swear the arrogant bastard had a smirk on his face when he walked out that door. Too bad. He can forget it. We aren't in high school. Hell, I'm too old to play games. And he's too old, period.*

Lily finished restocking and joined Joanie, cleaning the tables. Most of the patrons were gone, except for the two finishing up a game of pool. Relieved to see Brock had already left, she hoped to leave before Joanie pestered her with questions. *Too late*, Lily thought when she saw the determined look on Joanie's face.

"I saw Brock go into the storeroom when you were stocking the bottles," Joanie said. "When he came back out, it was obvious he didn't score with you. In fact, he went right on out the front door. What in the world did you do?"

"Nothing, absolutely nothing. And for future reference, it'll always be nothing. Grr."

The women laughed. Joanie loved to tease her friend. It was all in good fun. At times, Joanie was on the receiving end of the banter.

Finally, with the bar ready for business the next day, the three friends toasted to a new and exciting year. Lily prepared to leave. Ernie offered to walk her home since it was the wee morning hours, but Lily declined. Joanie agreed that Lily was quite capable of taking care of herself.

The cold air practically smacked her in the face. She walked fast. The moonlit night, the ocean ripples, and the quiet atmosphere made her think of the short time she had spent with Max. She remembered how he had held her hand as they walked the beach, like young lovers. She thought about the raw passion they'd shared in the lifeguard shack. *I miss him so much.*

As she approached her cottage, she saw a shadow of a man standing on her patio. At first, she thought it was Max. It wasn't, unfortunately. "What the hell are you doing here, Brock?"

"Now wait a minute, Lily. It's not what you think. Whether you like it or not, I'm really your friend. There are things I'm not able to tell you. Suffice it to say, Max should not have involved you in his mess. You need to move on. Max is dangerous; I know that first-hand."

"Well, to begin with, Mr. Savage, I will not be controlled by you or anyone else, ever again. So, you can't scare me. Furthermore, my relationship with Max is none of your damn business. Whether he comes back or not should be of no concern to you. I can take care of myself." Lily felt the heat rise in her face. She'd never felt so powerful.

"OK, I've warned you, even tried to be nice about it. I'll be around for awhile. Tonight, you didn't want my sexual prowess, but given time, you'll come running to me." He reached out to touch her.

Lily backed away. "Get over yourself, Brock. Go! I've had enough of you."

Brock turned to leave. "Honey, you haven't had me the first time, yet." He laughed.

She went inside, slamming her door purposely. Wasting no time, she climbed in bed, determined to erase her night's encounter with Mr. Arrogance. *He thinks he's God's gift to women*, Lily thought, shaking her head. *Sex Toy.*

Chapter 17

After a fitful night of sleep, Lily woke with a pounding headache, not from drinking too much alcohol, but from stress due to Brock's arrogance and thinly veiled threats. She looked in the mirror, seeing a frowsy old woman behaving like a teenager. *Shame on me. Here I am, pining away for a man I hardly know. Maybe Brock is right, Max won't be back. Well, I've lived through worse things. It's time I get on with my life. I'm just going to make Max a memory and leave it at that.* Her headache faded after some buttered toast and two cups of coffee. She quickly showered and dressed warmly, hoping to improve her mood with bright colors. Her list of resolutions for the New Year, which she'd made after all, was topped with exercising a positive attitude.

The shops were not open in Eagle Hills, North Carolina on New Year's Day. Earlier, the town council decided it was a time to be with family. Never much of a drinker, Lily often embarrassed herself when she drank wine or vodka. Living a protected life in the mountains, she didn't really fit in with the baby boomer generation. Joanie, however, was Lily's alternate self. Having plenty of experience in men, partying, and alcohol, Joanie always lived on the edge.

Sitting in her overstuffed recliner, Lily turned the pages of the *Eagle Hills Gazette*. Ready to fold the paper for the recycling bin, she noticed something on the back page in small print, an update on the murder of Jane Lawson. *It's a shame that it's taking so long to find the killer. There's no doubt in my mind that somebody is keeping secrets.* The short article indicated that forensics had found a partial set of fingerprints and were active in confirming the identity.

The police were following several leads. *I wonder if this was written to try to draw out the killer.*

With nowhere to go and nothing exciting to do, Lily sat down at her Singer sewing machine and lightly placed her foot on the pedal. *Oh, I remember my Granny sitting for hours at her machine, making dresses for the women and shirts and pants for the men in our family. She always let me sew, even if it wasn't anything important, maybe just a straight line. I was so proud. I miss her, even now.*

The rest of the day Lily spent reading, napping, and watching old black and white movies. She cried at *Casablanca* and covered her eyes watching *The Birds*. She didn't mind being by herself. Certainly not a chef in her tiny mansion, she opened a can of soup, nuked it in her used microwave, and crumbled a half of a package of stale saltines into the bowl to soak up the broth.

The phone never rang. She didn't expect it to, although she still held on to the possibility that Max would call. By 9 p.m., Lily was back in bed. When she reached over to grab the book on her nightstand, she realized it was Brock's novel. *Well, crap, I've read a third of the story. I might as well read the rest. It might put me to sleep. I hate to admit it, but he's a pretty good writer. I'd never tell him that, though. Not now that I know how overinflated his ego already is.*

When the morning light gleamed through her window, the book was still laying on the bed. Before drifting off to sleep, her imagination had matched the story of a secret military mission going awry. She wondered if all Brock's books weaved a true story into the plot. Lily threw back the covers and stumbled into the kitchen to make her coffee, then heated up a stale honey bun. Breakfast was ready.

By the time she'd dressed, Lily had decided to check up on Beverly at her lingerie boutique. Usually Beverly hosted a huge New Year's Eve party at her mansion, but not this year. It seemed like Beverly had suddenly become more of a recluse, the opposite of her previously brash, outgoing persona that most folks either adored or feared. Besides, Lily hoped to get some more info on Brock—and no doubt, Beverly knew everything about that man. According to earlier conversations over several glasses of wine, Brock hadn't missed his sexcapades with Beverly in years.

Lily made a quick walk to the boutique before noon. She figured Beverly would lock up for lunch, giving her a great opportunity to get some questions answered. However, when she approached the door, there was a *Closed* sign hanging in the door. *That's strange. I wonder if she's ill. She's always in the shop. Her house isn't far; I think I'll go check on her.*

After Lily rattled the door just to make sure it was secured, she hurried up the path to Beverly's home. On the wrap-around porch, she noticed all the window shades had been pulled. She rang the doorbell several times, with no response. She knocked hard, then pounded with her fist. Finally, the door creaked open.

Lily still couldn't see who was behind the door. "Beverly, it's Lily. Are you OK?

"I'm fine. Now please, leave me alone."

Lily felt concerned. "Honey, can I come in? I missed you on New Year's."

There was a moment of uncomfortable silence. "OK, come on in. I said I was fine."

Lily tried to hide her shock from seeing her beautiful friend in such a state of disarray. Instead of perfectly coiffed hair and meticulously put together attire, Beverly looked as if she hadn't bathed or changed clothes in days. Lacking makeup as well, she appeared much older and definitely in distress.

Beverly led Lily into the large living room, filled with antiques and heavy drapery. It was a different look than when she was there for the Halloween party. Lily made herself comfortable on the couch while Beverly sat in a hardback chair.

Lily kept the conversation light and easy; she felt it wasn't the time to ask about Brock. During their chat, Lily noticed that Beverly was nervously picking at a loose piece of yarn on her sweater. "Honey, I can see you got a lot on your mind. I'll be glad to listen if you need to talk. I promise to keep your troubles to myself," Lily said.

Tears streamed down Beverly's ashen cheeks. Lily motioned for Beverly to sit on the couch with her.

Beverly shook her head. "I can't. I can't sit on that couch...ever. I *hate* that thing."

"OK. Just tell me what's wrong," Lily said. "I can see you're upset."

Beverly burst into tears again. "I can't talk about it. He says if I open my mouth, I'll go to prison for the rest of my life."

"Now look here. First of all, I can't think of anything you could do to put you in jail. Second, who is this man who's threatening you?" Lily raised her voice, upset.

"My brother." Beverly sat up straight in her chair and cleared her throat.

"Who's your brother? I didn't know you had a brother."

There was a slight hesitation. Then, Beverly let loose, rambling between sobs. "Lily, Senator John Butcher is my brother. We were adopted at birth. We never knew about each other until a few years ago. John thought it was best to keep it a secret. He didn't want the media to rip it apart and shade his chances of getting elected. He's taken good care of me, buying this house, my car, the Harley. He even gave me money to buy the boutique. But now, I don't know what's going to happen."

"None of this would end you up in prison. This is just family stuff."

"Lily, I promised John never to speak a word of it. He would get very angry at me if he knew I told you, especially in his condition. This is not a good idea."

"What do you mean?"

"John is staying up north at his cabin up in the Adirondacks...recovering. We've kept the media in the dark. They think he's enjoying himself on a well-deserved vacation and working on his campaign plans. His chances for re-election are looking good; he doesn't need any bad publicity."

"I didn't know the Senator had a drug problem."

"Oh no, he doesn't. He was in his office working late one night. An intruder broke in, shot him, and just left him there. John called his personal physician, who went to John's office. The bullet's entry and exit left a clean wound through his foot. With John's resistance to going to the hospital, the doctor bandaged his wound and gave him antibiotics to prevent infection. Then, my brother called his pilot to take him in his private plane to Saranac Lake in the Adirondacks, where he owns a cabin. He rented a car for the rest of the way. The news reporters hounded Sheri relentlessly as to his whereabouts, but she is very protective of her husband. I expect you not to tell anyone what I have said. It's just too important."

"I promise, I won't say a word. How's his wife doing?"

"She's wonderful. We think John should be back home soon."

"Beverly, I still don't understand. Why are you afraid you might go to jail?"

"Uh, well... Yeah. You're right. I guess I got all confused. I'm just so worried. Don't pay any attention to me."

"Now you know if there's anything you need, you can call on me. I mean that. You've been very good to me, especially when I first came into your shop. I was so naïve. I'd never owned any intimate wear before moving here. When you let me see your pink room with all those toys on display, you were very patient with me. Oh, guess what! I certainly enjoyed the pink fuzzy handcuffs. I guess I lived in the dark ages until now." Lily broke the tension.

They laughed at that, and Lily offered to work at the boutique if Beverly needed more time to get her life back together. *I know she isn't telling me everything. That's OK. Some things come slowly.*

"Changing the subject, I wanted to know more about that man named Brock Savage. I mean, him as a person, not a naked author," Lily said.

"Oh, Brock...that silver-torgued devil. He's someone I would trust with my life. He can be a pain in the ass sometimes, but with his background and knowledge of the military, I feel very comfortable telling him anything. We are just good friends—OK, friends with benefits. That's all. He's one who will never get serious about a relationship. Why do you ask?"

"He came on to me at Ernie's on New Year's Eve. Later, he said some things that pissed me off. I got the idea that he knew too much about me."

"Lily, he knows a lot about everyone in Eagle Hills, and beyond. Whatever he says, you can take it to the bank. If he's coming on to you, be flattered. If you don't want him, put him in his place. He'll eventually back off."

"Don't worry." Lily laughed. She reached over and hugged Beverly. "Don't get up. I'll let myself out. Be sure to call me if you need anything."

"I will. Thanks so much for coming. You've really made me feel better. Guess I did need to talk to someone."

Lily left the mansion. *A promise is a promise. I won't tell anyone what she said.* Walking briskly back to her cottage, she tried to assure herself that Brock wanted only a romp in bed, possibly seeing her as a conquest, but nothing else. She decided to ignore his gameplaying. *He ought to mind his own business and stay out of mine.*

Chapter 18

With only a wilted head of lettuce, half a jar of grape jelly, and a fungus-covered tomato in the house, Lily decided on a trip to Cheryl's Diner for an early dinner. Dark clouds in the distance over the ocean appeared to be stirring something evil. By the time she arrived, she felt the first stings of icy rain pellets.

"Get yourself in here, honey. There's a storm brewing," Cheryl said. "Hang your wet coat over there, next to the door, so it can dry. I'll bring you a cup of coffee."

"Thanks, Cheryl. I didn't think I'd get caught in it," Lily said. She took her coat off and hung it on the coat rack, then slid into a booth. "What's the special for today? I'm a bit hungry."

"Fried Chicken, mashed potatoes, corn, homemade rolls, and chocolate cake. Can I fix you a plate?" Cheryl placed the steaming cup of coffee in front of Lily.

"Oh, you bet you can!"

The diner was nearly empty. Lily had experienced the hectic lunch hour before and was relieved that she had come mid-afternoon. Although Cheryl wasn't free to join her for even a brief conversation, she enjoyed her meal alone. Before her last bite of chocolate cake and second cup of coffee, the rain ceased and the wind calmed. Sitting beside a window, she entertained herself by watching a mother attempting to keep her toddler from splashing in a puddle. She observed a young couple holding hands strolling past the diner, all smiles. It brought to mind one starry night when Max had walked her home. She missed him.

Lily paid her bill, put on her coat, and waved to Cheryl, who was busy preparing for the five o'clock crowd. Feeling a bit lonely, Lily stopped by the bookstore to chat with Debra and check out the new arrivals. She didn't expect to see Brock behind the counter.

"It seems I run into you everywhere I go. Are you thinking about taking up residence here in Eagle Hills?" Lily asked.

"Hello yourself, Lily. Don't be so testy. Debra had a dental appointment, so I offered to keep the shop open until she gets back. I can be a good friend if given a chance," Brock said. "Now, can I help you?"

"No. I was going to check out any new arrivals, but I can come back later."

"No need. I have the list right here. I'll show you where the new books are. Some aren't even on the shelf yet. I haven't had a chance to put them out."

Lily followed Brock through the store to the end of the second aisle. He pointed to a small stack of books on a shelf above her head. "These are the books that came in this morning," he said. "Do you want me to get them down for you?"

Before Lily could answer, Brock turned to face her. He was so close she could feel his breath. He caught her off guard when he slipped his arm around her waist and drew her closer. He grinned down at her, looking smug.

She reached down and grabbed his genitals. She stared up into his face with determination. "Let me go, *now*, or you're going have a hard time walking out of here."

"Damn it, Lily! You sure as hell are difficult," Brock muttered. "OK!"

Brock released her, and she did the same to him. Without another word, he went back up to the counter. Furious, Lily hurried out, slamming the door shut as she left. *I just don't get it. I'm beginning to think he's never been turned down before. Do I act desperate or something? Hell! I'm going home.*

Once inside her cottage, the tears flowed. She wasn't sure why. Lily felt lost, confused, and lonely. She hated it; she couldn't understand why she couldn't just get Max out of her mind, out of her heart. Maybe it was just a

112

fling, a brief interlude. She even tried to talk herself into being flattered that another man wanted her. It didn't work. She went to bed early, not because she was tired, but because she wanted to lie there hugging her pillow.

At 2 a.m., the phone rang. Startled out of a deep sleep, she grabbed the phone and yelled, "What? What do you want?"

"Lily, I'm sorry. I wanted to tell you..." Max said.

She thought she was dreaming. "Max? Is that you?" She sat up straight in the bed and threw the covers off.

"I miss you. Please don't give up on me. I'll explain later," Max whispered.

"Please come back soon. I miss you too."

The call disconnected. Lily was wide awake now. *Now what? He didn't sound like he was in trouble. He sounded sad or something. Oh, I wish he was here! He's not dangerous, and he isn't going to hurt me. Nothing Brock says about Max is going to make me second guess how I feel about him.* Lily snuggled down under the covers once again. This time, sleep came quickly. She felt comforted, knowing Max cared for her.

In the morning, Lily bounced out of bed with newfound energy. She drank coffee and munched on saltine crackers smeared with grape jelly, calling it breakfast. With no agenda or project in mind, she began her day by stopping in the lingerie shop to check on Beverly. Although it was about fifteen minutes before opening, she found the door unlocked. She figured Beverly was in the back of the store.

When Beverly failed to come out front to greet her, Lily walked back to the secret pink room, assuming she was putting up stock. Only a few knew about the back room. Seeing that Lily was ill-informed about sexual pleasure early on, Beverly had taken her aside and urged her to explore her sexuality. With Max in her life, Lily had blossomed into a sensual being, taking advantage of Beverly's merchandise.

Lily felt déjà vu as she stepped through the doorway of the pink room. There in front of her was Brock, sitting in a chair, with Beverly straddling him. Still somewhat clothed, she was pumping him hard and fast. His pants were crumpled down around his feet. They were so caught up in the throes of ecstasy that they didn't even notice Lily standing there. After the obvious oohs and aahs, it was apparent the sex act was finished. Lily stepped inside.

"Well, friends, seems like I've been in this situation before," Lily said.

Without getting off of Brock's lap, Beverly looked over at the door to see they had an audience. "Hi, Lily. So nice of you to drop in."

"Again, I'm sorry. The front door was unlocked, so I came on in," Lily said. "Hello Brock. Nice to see you again. Oh, don't bother getting up." She grinned.

Brock nodded, his face wearing an expression of aggravation. He was literally stuck in a chair with a woman sitting on his spent manhood. If Beverly rose up off of him, the view would not be pretty. So, he kept his arms around her as the two women talked.

"Honey, I really thought the front door was locked. But no matter, I'm happy to see you," Beverly said. "If you'll do me a favor and go out front in case a customer comes in, I'd really appreciate it. I'll be there in just a few minutes."

Lily looked at Brock, who was staring at the wall. She wanted to laugh but refrained, not wanting to make Beverly feel uncomfortable. "Sure, I'll wait for you at the counter." She turned to leave. "Oh, Brock, always a pleasure to see you." *I'll bet his magic sword is shriveled now.*

Beverly joined Lily at the counter just as a customer came in the store. Lily could hardly look at Beverly without smiling. When the customer paid for her merchandise, Brock walked through the store without even a glance at the women.

"Good morning, ladies. Thank you, Beverly, for assisting me in my endeavor. I will be in touch," Brock said, reaching for the doorknob. He gave a half-hearted salute before strutting down the sidewalk.

Beverly couldn't maintain her composure any longer. The uneasiness between two friends disappeared when Beverly burst out laughing. Although the customer didn't have a clue about what had just occurred, she joined in on the laughter. Nothing was said or explained. It was one of those times when words couldn't possibly make it any better.

After the customer left, Lily told Beverly she was glad she was obviously feeling better and reminded her to call if she needed anything. Beverly thanked her and told her that the senator would soon be returning. She seemed happy about that, but Lily could tell there was something else both-ering her. Not wanting to give Beverly any more stress, she decided to leave well enough alone. She figured Beverly would tell her in time—and if not, it would still be OK.

Later that afternoon, Joanie called Lily with an invitation to a surprise birthday party for Ernie that night. Joanie explained that it was a spur-of-the-moment get-together, rather than a carefully planned party because it was nearly impossible to keep anything from Ernie. She said it was a very casual event, no gifts.

"I just want to have some of his close friends and lots of laughs. That's all. I'm ordering pizzas from Bob's because he's the best. So please, just come as you are, around seven o'clock," Joanie said.

"OK, I'll be there. That's really sweet of you, Joanie. I know he cares a lot for you," Lily answered. "I can see it in his eyes when he looks at you."

"Yeah, I thought I would never feel this way, but he really makes me happy. At this stage in my life, I thought all that was behind me and I would die alone."

"Trust me, there's been times I felt like that, too. I've changed my atti-tude, though; now, I feel there's always hope for a wonderful future. It may not be a long future, but it just might be the happiest," Lily said.

"Whoa, girl! You've really changed! We're going to have a long talk soon. Seems like I may have missed some stuff going on with you."

After they hung up, Lily rummaged through the kitchen pantry for any-thing resembling unexpired food. Finding a can of chicken noodle soup, she happily nuked it and sat down to her supper. She made a mental note to go to the grocery store soon. She hated shopping; Lily always felt worse after trips to buy food. It really wasn't a matter of finances; she simply thought it was a shame and disgrace to see food prices set so high that it caused hard-ships on families. Food is a staple, necessary for life, and should be free for everyone, in her opinion.

Lily took a quick shower, then stared into her closet for several minutes, trying to decide what to wear to the party. Casual wear was pretty much all that hung in her closet. After changing clothes twice, she finally settled on a pair of navy blue pants and a white v-neck long-sleeved top. Looking in the mirror, she was equally proud and embarrassed. With the low v-neck reveal-ing part of her ample breasts, she felt sexy in a suggestive sort of way. *Am I brave enough to wear this? I guess I've lost some weight. It kind of looks nice. Yep, I'm going to wear it.*

Lily arrived at Ernie's a few minutes early, thinking Joanie might need some help with preparations. Joanie told Ernie the bar was running low on rum and sent him to the liquor store to buy a couple of fifths to do until she could call in an order the next day. Actually, she had hidden two bottles of Captain Morgan behind a shelf in the stock room. She just needed to get him out of the bar to gather the patrons for his surprise birthday party. It worked out well; with Lily's help, Joanie quickly set up a table with deco-rations, bowls of chips, nuts, and mints. Bob brought the pizzas right on time. When Ernie came back with the rum, there were at least fourteen of his friends breaking into the Happy Birthday song, singing loudly and very much off-key.

The party kicked into full gear when Ernie's favorite local band, The Travelers, made a surprise entrance. With music from the '60s and '70s blaring, everyone filled the small dance floor. Lily caught Ernie mouthing the words "I love you" to Joanie as the newest member of the band, Marla, sang a love song.

As the party wound down close to 11 o'clock, the band loaded their equipment back into their van, drank one last beer, and said their good-byes. Ernie thanked them and asked them back for another performance in a couple of weeks. Joanie shook the lead guitar player's hand, slipping him a hundred-dollar bill. He tried to give it back, but she insisted. The entire band had been friends with Ernie for a long time. They had offered to play for free when Joanie contacted them.

Lily didn't mind walking home late at night. She liked the cold air, hav-ing drank more than her usual two bourbons. By the time she got inside her cottage, she was ready to go to bed. She crawled between the sheets, naked and restless. She wanted to feel the ecstasy she enjoyed with Max. Even as she reached down and manipulated her womanhood, it only brought frus-tration. She stopped, rolled over, and eventually fell asleep.

Around 1 a.m., she was awakened by knocking on her front door. Startled, she grabbed her pistol and hurried to the door. She peeked out the front window. In the dark of night stood the man who had created a world of desire that she never knew existed.

She opened the door. "Max," she whispered.

Without a word, he stepped inside, took the gun from her hand, and laid it on the end table. He was drawn so intensely to this hot-blooded woman who turned his world upside down. He took her in his arms, bent down, and kissed her softly. She trembled. He responded, kissing her fiercely, with a raging passion. She was not ashamed, nor embarrassed. She slid her hand down to his crotch. Feeling his large hardness, she rubbed it gently through his clothing. He gasped.

Lily led him to her bedroom. She decided if all of this was a dream, she was going to make it the best she'd ever had, one to remember. She started to speak, but Max put his finger against her lips and shook his head. For whatever reason, words were not needed or wanted. That was fine with Lily.

Still standing, he stripped off his clothing. Then, he slowly undressed her, paying special attention to her mound. His fingers felt the wetness between her legs. He slipped his middle finger into his mouth, licking her juice. He turned her around, her back against his chest. He reached around to cup her heaving breasts, tweaking her nipples. With the tip of his tongue, he gently touched the back of her neck, trailing kisses down her shoulder.

Lily wanted to be the dominant one. She wanted to take him right then, to ride him until he was spent. That was not his plan, though. For weeks she had imagined this night. Yet, her plan for their roles was reversed; he unleashed his passion to ensure she felt the pinnacle of ecstasy. She crawled onto the edge of the bed, staying on her hands and knees. Max approached her bare ass and spread her cheeks. With his hot hard rod, he entered her wet passage. He didn't hesitate, driving his tool to its hilt. He was the master. She cried out. Their intense urges created an all-consuming lust. Nothing else mattered. When he felt her muscles squeeze his manhood, he knew she was ready. He pumped her hard and fast. She felt him filling her up as they rose together in a powerful union.

Afterwards, Lily lay in his arms, motionless, not wanting the moment to end. She felt safe, loved, and most of all, she felt complete.

Finally, Max kissed her on the cheek, breaking the spell. "Lily, I...I..." he hesitated.

"It's OK." She rubbed his arm gently. "There will be another time. We'll talk when you are ready. Please, just be careful."

He eased himself away from her, feeling her seductive, curvy body. Her sultry eyes captivated him. He placed his lips against her inviting mouth for a kiss that was deliberately soft, slow, and meaningful. His mind was racing; Max knew he needed to get out of there...that he had to leave her to keep her safe.

Lily didn't pressure him for any answers when he left the bed and dressed. She slipped her robe on, understanding that he had to leave. When he kissed her on the forehead as he had done many times before, she smiled. "Someday," she said.

"Yes. Someday," Max replied.

Lily watched him disappear into the night, then returned to bed and relived their hours of passion. She wept, trying to find reason within her confused state of mind. She knew she didn't want her life to return to what it had been before Max. Yet, she didn't want to have him inconsistently and unexpectedly appear at her doorstep; the uncertainty was too stressful. *I'm too old for this. I'm trying to be patient, but time is not on our side—not at our age.*

She snuggled down between the covers. Her body relaxed as she listened to the pings of rain against the window.

Chapter 19

Max raced through the cold rain to his truck, which he had hidden several hundred yards away from the road, near a line of oak trees. He realized the chance he took coming back to Eagle Hills to hold his Lily in his arms once again. He couldn't keep living this way. *The senator will be coming back here in a few days. I think it's a stalemate. He knows I will destroy his political career if he opens his mouth. So far, I've not seen any of his henchmen since that night.*

As he drove back to the RV campsite he called home, the two-lane road seemed much longer than thirty miles. Although he was accustomed to moving to a new location at a moment's notice, now it had become a burden. Lily changed his world. He craved stability with his woman; he desperately wanted some kind of normalcy.

When he opened the camper door, Max froze, not knowing whether to run or fire his pistol. Sam didn't seem to be bothered by this woman sitting in a chair and holding a drink. Max jumped back, thinking he was seeing Jane's ghost.

"How in the hell did you get in here?" Max yelled. He reached into his jacket and pulled his gun. "Who are you?"

"Hey, wait a minute. Don't shoot me. I'm Jane's sister."

Max went in, slammed the door, and towered over her with his hand still on his gun. "Jane never told me she had a sister, much less a twin. What are you doing here?"

"Look, my name is Jessie. Either there's a bunch of bozos on my sister's case, or there's someone not telling everything. I'm here because the whole thing stinks. It reeks of a cover-up. It's been months with no one brought in for questioning, much less an arrest. I'm not going to let Jane's killer just disappear," Jessie said. "I know about you and Jane, back in the day. She thought the world of you. I work for the agency too, but in a different capacity. It wasn't hard to track you down. This place isn't too bad; you've definitely stayed in a lot worse." She took a gulp of her drink. "I didn't know how long you were going to be at Lily's, so I kind of made myself at home. Didn't think you would mind."

Max just stood silently, calculating his next step. He didn't know exactly what this woman expected. *Damn, you're creepy. You look just like Jane.*

"Lighten up, for heaven's sake! I'm not going to hurt you," Jessie quipped.

Max laid his gun down on the kitchen counter. "I know damn well you aren't." His anger rose, his face flushed. "How in the hell do you know about Lily? Does everyone in the whole agency follow me around? She doesn't have a damn thing to do with Jane's death, or anything I'm involved in. She's innocent—and that's the way it's going to stay. Leave her out of this!"

"You know we can't ignore her. You brought her into your life. We have a twenty-four hour detail on her. She's safe—well, for now."

"What else is going on that I don't know about?"

"Nothing that I can talk about right now. Besides, finding my sister's killer is my priority. The other shit can wait."

Careful not to turn his back on the woman who had broken into his home, Max reached into the refrigerator for a small jar of liquid containing a slice of apple. He filled a shot glass, turned it up, and swallowed.

"I see you're still making your famous apple pie moonshine," Jessie said.

"I don't know about famous, but it's pretty good. Now, I'm not sure what you want out of me, but right now I'm tired. So, how about leaving? Because I'm going to bed."

"Aw, come on! I don't have any place to stay for tonight. I figure the least you could do is offer the couch."

"Oh, *goody!* Now I have a roommate!" His voice was dripping with sarcasm. He sighed, then tossed Jessie a pillow and quilt from the tiny closet. "OK, just for tonight. Here, make your bed."

"Thanks! I just knew you were a good guy." Jessie laughed.

Max grabbed his gun and motioned for Sam to follow him back into his bedroom. He yelled back to Jessie. "Don't forget to turn out the lights and lock the damn door."

"Yes *sir*!"

Even though there was a stranger sleeping in his living room, Max had no trouble sleeping. He was tired. *I just ain't a young man anymore.*

The aroma of fried bacon woke him up. Looking at his clock, Max growled, "Six a.m.!" He rolled out of bed and stumbled into the little kitchen, getting a clear picture of Jessie standing at the counter, eating a hefty breakfast. He rubbed his eyes.

"Now you're eating my food? Do you always just take over when you're in a stranger's home?" he asked.

"Well, huh... Now that you mention it, yes, I do! I take care of myself." Jessie answered. Then, she dramatically stuffed a forkful of scrambled eggs into her mouth.

Max shook his head. Realizing he was only wearing his briefs, he went back to the bedroom and slipped on a pair of ragged shorts. When he returned to the kitchen, there was a plate of bacon, eggs, and toast waiting for him on the counter.

"Here!" she said, handing him a glass of water. "There's no juice or milk, and it's a bit too early for liquor."

He didn't waste any time; he ate as if he was starved. "Are you always so bossy?"

"Yeah, I guess so."

After being plied with food, he knew the interrogation would begin momentarily. He soon realized Jessie was no dummy. She wasn't as quick as Jane, but he could see a lot of the same mannerisms and behaviors. Jane's area of expertise was manipulation. She could weave her questions into innocuous conversation in such a way that she always got what she needed. Jane stirred the pot until she was satisfied with the results. Jessie tried, but she just wasn't good enough. He didn't reveal all he knew about Jane's death, but he did give her snippets—such as that he heard Jane was in Eagle Hills to warn him about possible dangers. Jessie didn't offer any new information in return. It seemed all their answers were carefully orchestrated. Neither one wanted to give up any details.

"I've talked to the police and the coroner. There were no eyewitnesses, or let's just say, no eyewitnesses have come forward. Jane wasn't sexually assaulted. It wasn't robbery because she still had her jewelry, and her billfold was in her pocket. I find it odd that she was barefoot, but they also said she'd been killed somewhere else and left on the beach. It was in the paper that the police have a partial set of fingerprints, so I'm hoping that will break the case. I figure it was a surprise attack because she was hit in the back of the head. If she had been approached directly, I know for a fact my sister would have done some serious damage," Jessie declared.

"I agree with you." Max made his answers brief. "In all honesty, Jessie, I wish I knew more. I want to put all this chaos to rest. I want a life of my own—but I doubt that will ever happen. Jane was a very good friend, and I cared for her a lot. We worked well together; we could practically read each other's minds. If I can be of any help in solving this, I won't hesitate to let you know." *I wish she would just leave. I can't say any more than what I have said.*

"Thanks for letting me stay overnight. I really appreciate it. Your lumpy couch actually felt good," Jessie replied. "I'm going to be staying at the inn in Eagle Hills. I don't feel I can leave until I get some answers, for my peace of mind and the memory of my sister."

"Have you got transportation?"

"Yeah, my jeep is parked a couple of streets over, near a gas station. I left it there because I didn't want you to freak out when you came home last night, seeing a strange vehicle out front."

"Aw hell. That doesn't compare to opening the door and seeing the spitting image of Jane sitting in my living room. Damn, you nearly gave me a heart attack." Max laughed.

"I'm really sorry. I didn't even think of that. Anyway... I'm going to leave now, but I'll be in touch." Jessie gave Max a quick hug. "Thanks for everything."

"You're welcome. Don't worry, I have a feeling that we'll be running into each other. It's a small place."

After Jessie left, Max sat in his recliner, trying to make sense of the last twenty-four hours. He wished he knew who killed his friend. He really couldn't get involved in solving that mystery, since he was forced to stay under the radar. It bothered him somewhat that Jane had never mentioned she had a twin sister. But then, there was never really a good time for them to discuss relatives and childhoods. It gave him chills thinking about how much Jessie and Jane looked alike.

Sam nudged his master, bringing her leash and laying her paw on his knee. Max laughed. "I'm sorry, Sam. There's just so much that's been happening. Come on, let's go out," he said.

Fortunately, no one was outside as the two took their walk. The RV community was small, with less than fifteen permanent residents. Trees surrounded the camp, which made it a perfect hideaway. A little pond provided an enjoyable spot for gatherings and cookouts, but Max just wasn't in the mood to chat. He preferred to stay a stranger; no neighbor need apply for a friendship. He was just getting tired of people in general. Sam was the perfect companion.

His life had always been complicated, even before joining the agency. His childhood had been spent in a dozen foster homes, with only one that took the time to show him some affectionate attention. Oddly, that was when he was a young boy, living on a farm in Ohio. He grew to enjoy caring for the animals as part of his chores. That family taught him responsibility, gave him security, and showered him with love. Walking back to his RV, he thought about Jane. He wished he had grown up with a sibling. He couldn't blame Jessie for trying to find her twin sister's killer.

After giving Sam a treat, Max took a hot shower. Wearing an old, thin, gray sweat suit, he settled into his recliner. *I hate having to stay inside. Hell, I can't even go play a round of golf. I'd even be satisfied with putt-putt right now. There's nothing to do! I think I'm going a little nuts just sitting here. I wonder what Lily's doing; maybe I'll call her later.*

"Sam, how in the world did I get in this mess? I'm supposed to enjoy retirement. I sure have earned it! I need to find out when the senator's coming back to town and stay on top of that. If he's got any sense at all, he'll shut the hell up and get off my back."

Max went outside to a small shed next to the RV. He rummaged around in boxes of the personal things that had been stored there for him. He'd never questioned who was in charge of moving his belongings. The agency did a good job of providing for him. As he was about to close up, he glanced over to a corner. He discovered a tackle box and a fishing pole left by the previous tenant. "Oh, look what we have here!" He checked it over and took it inside. "Sam, guess what? We're going fishing!"

The man and his dog fished in the little pond until late afternoon, never catching even a nibble. It didn't matter; it was the most relaxing, reflective time that Max had experienced in a long time. "Well, Sam, we've been here long enough. Guess it's time to go home. Come on, girl."

As the two walked back home, he noticed that someone had parked a Screamin' Eagle Street Glide just a few doors down from his RV. Max stopped abruptly, admiring the black Harley with nice saddlebags. The FOR SALE sign really captured his attention. *Hmm, that's a nice ride! I might check that out tomorrow. Depends on the price. I could go park it at Lily's and nobody would think anything about it. If things die down, maybe we could ride with Joanie and Ernie sometime. I need some joy in my life soon. I remember the bike I had back in the day was unbeatable. I kept the shine on that chrome so slick, it would blind you in the sun. I loved that ride. I miss that freedom.*

Chapter 20

While Max rummaged through his kitchen cabinets for something re-sembling an edible dinner, Lily was enjoying a succulent, medium-well sirloin steak in her kitchen. She'd spent most of the day painting the old bench in front of her cottage, taking advantage of the warm, sunny weather to stay outdoors. She didn't expect Max to call. He'd left on a good note, at least. She decided to just step back and let it just run its course.

When Lily painted something, she was always a hot mess by the time she was through. After she finished the bench and cleaned up, she wasn't in the mood to cook a meal. With a growling stomach, she hurried to Cheryl's for a country dinner. The booths were all full. Luckily, she found a stool at the counter.

"Wow, Lily, you're glowing. Anything or anyone you want to tell me about?" Cheryl enquired.

Lily took a sip of her sweet tea and smiled. "Oh, I was out in the sun working today. Maybe that's it."

"Oh, please! I think it's more than that. Anyway, you look really happy. I wish I could find some of that sunshine," Cheryl giggled. "Good for you!"

Lily's face beamed with contentment; she felt special. Although nothing about her involvement with Max was conventional, she found it captivating. Never having experienced such a complicated relationship, she felt charmed by its mystery and secrets. *I wish I was an author. I would write my life's story. It'd be called fiction; even though it's true, nobody would believe it*, she thought.

When she finished her meal, she left a generous tip on the counter for Cheryl. Lily believed in tipping, mostly because when she was a young woman, she had waitressed at the local cafe. She knew how difficult the job could be at times.

She stopped by the bookstore to pass some time. Finding Debra on a ladder, stacking some books on the top shelves, Lily stood guard at the counter. They chatted back and forth. Debra was always happy to have her help out. Lily enjoyed pretending to work there, even operating the register on occasion. Debra had offered her a part-time job, but Lily didn't want to be paid for having fun—and she certainly didn't want to have that obligation.

While Debra was checking some invoices in the back office, Lily sold several books—and even a couple of Brock Savage audiobooks. About an hour before closing, a woman came in asking for Brock Savage's newest mystery. Lily directed her to the section filled with all his books. She kept looking at the woman, trying not to be so obvious as to stare. *She looks so familiar,* Lily thought. *I've seen her somewhere...but where? It's not like I go a lot of places.*

The woman laid a book down on the counter and held out a twenty-dollar bill. Lily tried to make small talk while trying to figure out how she knew this woman. "Savage's books are very popular right now. We've been selling a lot of them. In fact, he's been here twice for personal book signings."

"Yeah, he's a very good writer. And he sure is good looking," the woman said.

Lily took the payment and gave her some change back. "My name is Lily Roberts. Are you a new resident? I don't mean to be rude, but it just seems that I have seen you before."

"I'm getting that a lot lately. Actually, my name is Jessie." *I know who you are, my dear Lily. While I was at Max's camper last night, he was in your arms. He must really have a thing for you because he's taking some big chances lately,* she thought. "My twin sister was murdered here in Eagle Hills a while back. Her name was Jane Lawson. Since it's still an open case and nobody has been charged with her death, I decided to see what's holding up the investigation."

"Oh, my! I am so very sorry. Her picture was in our local paper. Actually, she was found not too far from my cottage, down on the beach. I hope you get some closure soon."

"Thanks. You have a good afternoon. I'm staying at the inn for a few days, so I'll probably see you around. Eagle Hills has that small town atmosphere. It's nice."

Lily laughed. "Yeah, that's for sure."

Debra came out of the office carrying an armful of magazines. "Hey, Lily. Thanks for helping me out. Would you please do me a favor and arrange these new magazines on the rack?"

"No problem. I want you to meet Jessie; she's visiting right now. Maybe we can talk her into staying for a while," Lily said.

"Welcome, Jessie. Hope you enjoy your stay here. If I can be of any help to you, let me know. Nearly everyone around here has been in the store at one time or another, especially when I have a book signing event," Debra said.

"Thanks, Debra. It's good to meet you. I have already found a book I have been anxious to read, that new one by Brock Savage. I'll probably be up all night reading it," Jessie said. "I'll be going now. Nice to have met you both."

After watching Jessie walk across the street, Debra couldn't hold her tongue any longer. "OK, what's the deal? Why is she here in Eagle Hills? Nobody comes here without a purpose."

Lily laughed. "Get your sleuthing hat on, girlfriend. Remember that dead woman on the beach a while back? That was her twin sister. She's come here to solve the murder mystery."

"Oh, this could be exciting! Maybe we need to invite her to lunch—or better yet, let's invite her for a drink at Ernie's. I'll even buy the first round."

"Hey, that's not a bad idea. Since she doesn't know anyone around here, we could offer to help introduce her to some folks. And in the meantime, she could give us a heads-up on what she finds out about her sister's death."

"For heaven's sake, Lily! The next thing I know, you'll be packing a gun and hunting down the bad guys."

Lily laughed and hugged her purse as if protecting it. "Now, how do you know I'm not already doing that?"

"Oh, *sure* you are. Hey, why don't we run over to Ernie's?" Debra asked, collecting the money from the register. "I'll be done as soon as I put this in the safe."

"Sounds good to me. I haven't seen Joanie in a while, but I know she's been pretty busy with tending bar—and of course, tending Ernie," Lily said.

"It must be nice. Hell, it's been so long since I had any romance, I wouldn't know how to behave," Debra said.

"I thought you and Savage had a thing going." Lily was anxious to know for sure.

"Oh, it was just a spur-of-the-moment roll in the hay. Don't get me wrong; he's very good at what he does, and we're still friends," Debra explained. "There's just no lasting spark."

"Yeah, I heard that he enjoys variety. Maybe that's why he rubs me the wrong way. I don't know what it is about him. I guess I'm old fashioned."

"I think we're both old fashioned."

The two women laughed as they walked over to Ernie's Nest. They took a seat at the bar, and Joanie fixed their drinks. They noticed only a few other customers; the booths were empty.

"Ladies, long time no see," Joanie said. "Lily, I really am sorry I haven't been knocking on your door. Honestly, I've been so busy working. And Ernie has been renovating in the back, to make that room he never used into a pool room. We've got a couple of really nice pool tables in there now. You ought to check it out sometime. And since we took the old pool tables out of the dance area, there's a lot more space up front. It's going to bring in more business."

"Hey, that's OK, Joanie. I'm just glad you're here. When you get some time, call me and we'll make a point of getting together, even if it's just for a few hours," Lily said.

"Count me in too," Debra said. "It would be nice to just have a girl's night out. And if we decide to get out of Eagle Hills, there's a very nice restaurant about thirty miles from here. I'll drive."

"Sounds like a plan!" Joanie said. "I'll see what I can do."

Lily stood up. "I'll be right back; I'm going to check out that pool room." With a drink in her hand, she went into the newly-decorated pool room, unprepared to see what she found. Her new friend Jessie was leaned over the pool table, attempting to make a shot. Brock Savage was bent over behind her, his hands covering her breasts.

"Oh, what a surprise!" Lily said. "Hello, Brock. Guess you're teaching Jessie some moves," Lily quipped. "Good to see you again, Jessie."

Brock straightened up and stepped away from the table. It was a sight to see; his massive rod stood at attention in his pants, once again.

Lily smiled, trying not to laugh. *He looks like he's got a pole holding up a tent,* she thought. *Wonder if it ever collapses.*

Jessie completed her shot. "Hi, Lily. So, you know Brock?"

"Uh, no... Not really, at least not as well as some others. We just seem to run into each other a lot lately," Lily explained. "When your game is over, come and join us at the bar."

Jessie nodded. "It may be awhile, but thanks."

Lily returned to the bar, grinning from ear to ear. She whispered to Debra that Jessie was playing pool with Brock. "That's not all they're playing, trust me!" Lily said.

"I swear, I believe he's a sex maniac," Debra said. "I mean... At our age, there's nothing wrong with it, but you would think at some point he would give it a rest."

Joanie overheard the conversation. A glass slipped from her hand as she was drying it and broke. She laughed out loud. "Honestly, you two are just hilarious."

Debra and Lily waited fifteen minutes longer, but it was obvious that Jessie was having too much fun playing pool to be joining them for a drink. They paid their tab, promised Joanie that they would have a girl's night out very soon, and left. Each going their separate ways, they hugged and went home. It had been a long day. Lily didn't waste any time getting home and crawling between the sheets.

Chapter 21

Max woke up the next morning with Sam lying on his chest, her cold nose nudging his cheek. He sat up on the side of the bed and rubbed his damp face. "OK, girl, I take the hint. Did I sleep too late?" He looked at the clock. "Hey! It's still early. Can't you let an old man sleep in every once in a while?"

Sam whined and looked up at her master like a little child. Max scratched behind her ears and playfully ruffled her fur. He quickly dressed in old tattered jeans and a stained t-shirt, then fastened Sam's leash to her collar. Off they went for the morning walk.

As he walked by the Harley, he was glad to see it was still for sale. He knocked on the door of the RV beside the parked bike. After a quick introduction to the owner, Max checked out the bike. He took it for a quick ride around the park while Sam waited patiently for her master's return. With low mileage and the generous offer of two free helmets, a deal was made. Max now owned a Screamin' Eagle Street Glide. Like a kid at Christmas, he grinned from ear to ear as he rolled the bike home, Sam trailing behind. *Now I can go to Lily's, or anywhere. No one will know. I wonder if Lily would ride with me. I'll ask her. If she's never ridden, I'll teach her. It's not that hard. I've always been a safe rider—well, except for that one time in Italy, but that's a whole different story.*

It was a good day for Max. He left Sam in the RV snoozing while he played with his new toy. He rode the Harley for nearly three hours, stopping at various side markets and stores along the country roads. He remembered riding the Dragon's Tail in North Carolina and the excitement he felt when he made it to the end. He longed to feel Lily pressing against his back, her arms around him, holding on. There was just something so personal, so powerful, about being in control of that massive machine.

When he returned, he parked the bike behind his RV and chain-locked it to an oak tree. He winced as he walked, his legs cramping with each step into the RV. "Sam, it's been a long time since I got on a bike. Oh, I feel like an old man." Max laughed. "If I sit down here in my chair, I may not be able to get up!" He got a cold beer and stood at the kitchen counter. "Don't be mad at me, Sam. You'll always come first."

After finishing his beer, he slowly settled into his recliner. Sam finally laid her head in his lap, as if to forgive him for leaving without her. Within a few minutes, Max was snoring. Sam curled up beside the chair, joining her master in an afternoon snooze.

The nap didn't last very long, however. He was rudely awakened, startled by the sound of his cell phone. He wasn't accustomed to having many phone calls, day or night. It was Dixie.

"Max, how do you like your new digs?" Dixie asked.

"I swear, woman, you ain't never going to leave me alone," Max said. "What do you want now?"

"I hear that you got yourself a Harley. We had some good times on your bike, back in the day."

"Am I under a damn microscope?! Yeah, I got a Screamin' Eagle, and it's a beauty. I don't know how long I'll be stuck in this RV. I needed a distraction," Max said. "Why are you calling, honey?"

Dixie laughed. "OK, I'll get to the point. I thought about coming over but figured a phone call would be safer for now anyway. Your good friend has been recouping at his cabin in the Adirondacks ever since that night you—ahem—'visited' him. He's kept in close contact with his wife all this time, until the last few days. She doesn't know if something's wrong up there or not, but she says it is very unusual for him not to call. We've sent a couple of people to check it out. It could be that his cell service was down, or he broke his phone. We just don't know. I was instructed to notify you, that's all."

"Well, hell... Don't get your drawers in a wad. That piece of trash probably thinks he's going to sneak back into town like he's been on a retreat. Don't worry about me. I've got better things to do than yank his chain."

"I'll keep you informed, just in case. You never know what that man is thinking. You take care of yourself. You know I'm close if you need me."

"Thanks. Catch you later," Max said.

After they hung up, Max relived that night the gun went off. *If I had planned to kill him, I wouldn't have shot him in the foot. He's been a thorn in my side far too long. He doesn't deserve the air he breathes. If the voters only knew how crooked he is...*

Max called Lily and made a date for that night. He was anxious to see her reaction when he arrived on his bike. After taking Sam for a brief walk, he jumped in the shower. As he lathered up, he thought about Lily's soft lips on his manhood. *Stop that! Save it for later*, he thought. He dressed in jeans, a fitted t-shirt, and boots. *I'm going commando tonight. If things go like I'm hoping, she'll be sitting on my rod tonight.*

Lily heard a bike stop in front of her cottage and assumed it was Joanie. But when there was a knock on the door, she became suspicious. With her pistol behind her back, she opened the door. "Oh! Max, come on in."

"No, come outside. I want to show you something," he said, taking her hand.

"OK, wait just a second." Lily laid her gun on the end table.

Max laughed. "I've sure got to be careful around you. You're dangerous."

The full moon highlighted the brilliant chrome and curves of the Harley parked a few feet away. Max stood beside it as if posing for a motorcycle magazine. Lily agreed that it was a beauty.

"What I want to know is, will you ride with me?" he asked.

"Sure I will." Lily felt confidence in Max. "But I don't have a helmet. I won't ride without one. It's just a thing with me."

"No problem, I have an extra one." He got the spare out of his saddlebag and helped her put it on. Then, he fastened his own helmet.

Lily grabbed her keys, locked the front door, and climbed on the back of the Harley. Max felt her warm body pressing close to his back as she wrapped her arms around him. They took off into the darkness, feeling free and untouchable. The weather was perfect, the traffic was light, and the sound of the motor was stimulating. The vibration of the massive machine created an arousing interest in Lily. She hugged her man tightly. Max loved the control, the feeling of dominance. He took to the road like a master. He turned off the main road onto a single lane, leading to a small clearing surrounded by trees and brush. Three picnic tables encircled a rusty outdoor grill. He stopped and cut the motor. The moon provided minimal light, filtering through the trees. It was nature; the rustling leaves and crickets surrounded the little area.

Max reached back and squeezed Lily's thigh. "Get off the bike, babe. Take off your helmet." he said.

"OK." Lily eased down off the bike, removed her helmet, and stretched her legs. She wasn't sure what his intentions were, but she trusted him.

Still on the bike, Max reached for her, kissing her forcefully. Already full of desire, she responded. He lit a fire in her, a passion unfulfilled. Her hand found his rod, naked and hard. He grabbed the back of her head, guiding it downward until her lips touched a drop of nectar on the tip of his shaft. Her tongue savored his ambrosia. Her mouth sucked in rapid motion, craving to taste him once again. Max was out of control. With his hands fisted in her tangled hair, he cried out and filled her mouth. She swallowed, knowing she'd given him an overwhelming feeling of release.

Max was surprised, but pleased when his organ maintained an erect position. "Take off your jeans...now," he ordered. Max felt determined to take advantage of the moment.

To his delight, Lily removed all her clothing. She didn't take her eyes off of Max. He was mesmerized by her erotic beauty in the moonlight. He put his arm around her waist, lifting her as she straddled the bike facing him. He cupped her breasts as he kissed her, darting his tongue into her mouth. She leaned back a bit as he massaged her breasts and suckled her nipples. She lost all concept of reserve. She wanted all of him, to feel him inside her. She raised her body up and mounted his manhood, covering him in her hot, wet love juice. Lily's breath caught in her throat as Max pushed between her thighs. She gasped. As he watched her enjoy the ride, he felt the pressure build. He leaned forward, whispering in her ear, and buried his shaft deep in her wetness. She felt his pulsating shaft and squeezed her muscles. Without a word, they exploded into sizzling euphoria.

Lily laid her head on his chest, listening to his heart beating in a strong rhythm. Max closed his eyes. They were both spent. He cradled her in his arms, wanting desperately to tell her that he loved her. He felt he had nothing to offer her; his life had no future. She waited for him to speak, hoping he would tell her what she longed to hear. It didn't happen.

"Honey, maybe you ought to put your clothes on now. It's getting chilly." Max gave her butterfly kisses on her face.

Lily looked up at the man whom she loved. "Yeah, that's a good idea." She giggled.

After he helped her off the bike, he dismounted, adjusted his clothes, and zipped up his pants. She dressed quickly. Before leaving their secluded love nest, he slipped his arms around her. Their kiss was long and tender. The ride back to Eagle Hills was uneventful. After parking the bike in front of her cottage, he walked her to the door.

"Thank you so much for...well, everything. The evening was more than I could ever imagine," Lily said. "You are simply amazing." *Don't you know by now that I love you?*

"It is you who is amazing. Lily, I...I really enjoy being with you." Max tried to tell her how vulnerable he felt, but his fear cut him off. *I love you, Lily. I pray someday I can tell you how much you mean to me.*

Max left when Lily was safely inside. She turned on the living room light and peeked out the window, watching him ride away. After a quick shower, she climbed into bed, tired but happy. Just as she closed her eyes, her phone rang. She really didn't want to talk to anyone right then, but when she saw it was Beverly, curiosity got the best of her.

"Oh, Lily. I'm sorry that I'm calling so late, but I really need to talk to someone. Please forgive me," Beverly pleaded.

Lily sat up in bed. "What's wrong? You sound so upset. Are you all right?"

"No, I'm not all right. I'm about crazy! I think my brother is missing. You know, I told you he was up at his cabin? Well, he hasn't been in contact with any of his family for several days. That's not like him. I'm worried to death," Beverly said.

"Have you called the police?"

"I can't. John made it clear that we were to never call the authorities if anything happened," Beverly said. Her voice quivered. She began to sob.

"Honey, I'm so sorry. I hate you're going through this. Not knowing is so hard. But I think I would try not to think of the worst right now. He may have lost his cell phone, or the closest signal tower could be down. There are lots of reasonable things that could have happened. He could have accidently dropped his phone in the lake. The best thing you can do is be patient. Surely he'll be in contact soon."

"You're right, Lily. I get myself so worked up, and it's probably for nothing. He can take care of himself. I mean, it's not like he's really disappeared; we know where he is."

"Good. Get some sleep. I'll call you or come by your shop tomorrow. Everything will be OK. Don't let your imagination get the best of you, Honey."

Chapter 22

The next day, Lily still had Beverly on her mind. About noon, she called the boutique but got no answer. She called Beverly's cell phone and left a message. It wasn't like Beverly to not be available at one of the numbers. *I'm going to take my own advice and be patient.*

Late that afternoon, Beverly appeared at Lily's cottage. Surprised by her visit, Lily invited her in, and they sat at the kitchen table. Upset and distraught, Beverly revealed she had spent some time at the senator's house earlier. His wife had told her that two government investigators had traveled to the cabin to check on John.

"That's why I didn't get back to you. I wanted to see what was going on first," Beverly explained. "I'm just a nervous wreck."

"No wonder you're upset. I'm so sorry. Hopefully there's a very simple explanation, and he's fine. Can I get you something to drink?" Lily asked.

"Just a glass of water, if you don't mind. I should be going in a few minutes. I just wanted to stop by." Beverly's phone rang. "Excuse me, I need to take this call."

While Lily poured two glasses of water and sat back down, Beverly stepped into the living room to talk to the mystery caller. When Beverly walked back into the kitchen, her face was flushed and her hands trembling.

"Are you OK? Sit down here, right now, before you fall down," Lily ordered.

"That was Brock on the phone. He and somebody named Jessie are the ones up at the cabin looking for John. He said he would keep in contact with me. He really is a good friend. I didn't know he was on the government payroll. I mean, I knew he had connections, but I guess I've been kept in the dark about a lot of things," Beverly said. She took a drink of the cold water.

Hearing that Jessie was with Brock didn't surprise Lily. She felt sorry for Beverly on many levels. *There are too many secrets in Eagle Hills. It isn't easy to trust anyone,* Lily thought.

"Maybe it's a good thing that Brock is helping out. I mean, you know him well, so that should be some comfort," Lily suggested.

"Yeah, you're right. Thanks for lending an ear. I was about at the end of my rope! I haven't slept well since all this started. I'm going home to fix me a few bourbons and go to bed. I know it's early, but maybe I can catch up on my rest."

Lily walked her to the door. "Like I said before Beverly, if you need me, just give me a call."

"I will. If I hear any more, I'll let you know. Thanks." She hugged Lily and left.

After finishing her household chores, Lily munched on peanut butter and crackers for dinner, then went outside to enjoy the ocean view. She relived the night before, savoring the exploding passion she felt with Max. She shook her head, thinking of her life back in Tennessee. She couldn't imagine returning to the holler. She felt as if she'd blossomed, grown in so many ways, since moving to Eagle Hills.

Daylight slowly faded. Lily hadn't heard from Max, but she really didn't expect a call yet. She'd grown accustomed to his mysterious absences, although they were irritating at times. Just when she resolved that he'd never be a constant in her life, he re-entered the picture. Being a stubborn mountain woman, determined to focus on reality, she refused to imagine a perfect life with this man. The years spent with Joe had tainted any expectations of happiness, leading her to believe her lot in life was one of endurance. She laughed, thinking of how a tug of war with a dog named Sam had changed her entire world.

Lily sat on her newly-painted bench, watching the birds dip into the ocean for food, with no idea that her life was about to change forever.

* * *

Several miles down the road, Max was receiving a phone call that handed him his freedom.

"Max, this is official business, off the record. What I tell you cannot be repeated," Jessie said. "Do you understand?"

"Yeah, yeah... What is it?"

"Now you listen to me, you stubborn old coot! Brock and I are up at the senator's cabin in New York. I wanted you to be the first one to hear this."

"So, it's the two of you that were sent up there to find that son of a bitch! Surely you aren't going to tell me that you're a threesome now?"

"Will you just shut the hell up? I'm telling you that we found the senator. He's dead," Jessie said. "He died before we could get help. He isn't a pretty sight, all swollen and turning black. It's really isolated up here, and cellphone service is hit and miss."

"Really? Too bad."

"Brock is on his cellphone with the coroner. We're having his body sent back to Eagle Hills as soon as possible. His wife doesn't even know yet. Here's what happened..."

"OK, OK, I'll shut up. But I can't say I'm going to miss him," Max quipped. "That piece of shit made my life a living hell."

Jessie took a deep breath and began. "Things are going to change for a lot of people when this goes public. When Brock and I got up here, we found the cabin undisturbed. The door was unlocked, but there were no other warning signs. Nothing really out of place. His wallet and cell phone lay on the table. The senator just wasn't here. His rental car was locked. We walked to the edge of the lake and checked the dock, but found nothing. We scanned a few hundred yards into the wooded area, too, but came up with zilch. While we sat on the porch deciding on our next move, Brock heard a faint noise from behind the cabin. We went around back and there he was, sitting on the ground, propped up between the generator and a stack of cut wood. At first we thought he was dead; then, his eyes opened. He screamed, terrified. He thought he was seeing a ghost, my sister Jane. He said, "It can't be you! I dumped your body on the beach that night! You're dead!" He

138

started choking. That scared the devil out of me. I never expected this, not in a million years. His speech was slurred, his neck twice its normal size, and he couldn't move his swollen arm. We assured him he wasn't seeing things and that I wasn't Jane. I asked him how he got injured. He said his generator had stopped working, and he came out to check it. When he bent down to take the gas cap off, he put his hand on the stack of firewood. He said he felt a stab, jerked his hand away, and saw that he stood inches away from a timber rattler. His quick movement caused the snake to feel more threatened. It rose up and bit him again, this time on the neck. He was unable to tell us much after that. I think he'd been out there for more than a day. I told him we were getting help and to hang on. He kept mumbling, 'I'm sorry. I'm sorry. You didn't need to die.' Then, the son of a bitch died. He killed my sister and got away with it!"

"Damn it to hell! I figured he was involved, but there was no concrete proof, nothing I could run with. That low life got away with murder. Karma's a bitch, ain't it? At least there's some closure," Max said.

"You're right. All this will hit me later. Right now, his body bag is soon on a plane. It won't be easy facing his family. I don't look forward to that at all. I'll contact you later," Jessie said. "Don't breathe a word of this."

After they hung up, Max sat in his recliner for a long time, absorbing Jessie's story. Later, he took Sam for a walk, made sure her bowl was filled, and called it a night. He didn't bother with dinner. All the excitement churned in his stomach, making food an iffy proposition. Lying in bed, he realized that the weight was finally lifted. He was *free*, free to have a normal life. No more worry, no random moving at a moment's notice—not any more. Max sat up in bed, grabbed Sam, who was snuggled next to him, and kissed his best friend on her nose. "Oh God, Sam, it's over!"

The next morning, Max went fishing. He had to do something to contain his euphoria, to keep himself grounded until he figured out exactly what he wanted to do. Sam enjoyed pestering a rabbit on the bank of the pond while Max cast his line lazily, hoping to catch a big one.

His mind was filled with exciting possibilities. He desperately wanted his relationship with Lily to be a lot more than an interlude every few days. Now, just maybe he could have it all.

Max fought the urge to call Lily. He didn't want to see her until the news was out to the general public. He could never tell her about his work in specifics, could never reveal his connection to the senator. *Some things are better left with the dead,* he thought.

After he returned to the RV, he left Sam inside to nap while he took a quick ride on his new bike. This time he jacked up the speed, roaring down an empty highway. He felt the power of the motor, the wind in his face, and he was in love. Only a biker could understand.

Chapter 23

Lily's plans to have lunch with Debra were put on hold when Beverly called her, frantic again. She asked Lily to come to her house because Brock and Jessie were going to give her an update on her brother. Beverly hinted that she didn't want to be alone.

When Lily arrived, Beverly looked terribly pale. Her home, usually neat, showed a disturbing disarray. They chatted for a bit, and then, out of nowhere, Beverly burst into tears.

"I know something is wrong, Lily! They wouldn't be coming to talk to me unless it was bad. Oh, what am I going to do?" Beverly asked. "This can't be good!"

"Look, whatever it is, you'll deal with it. You aren't alone. You've got a lot of friends. Let's just wait and see. Your imagination is running away with you. Stop it, and take some deep breaths."

A knock on the door interrupted their conversation. When Beverly opened the door, the sight of Jessie was too much. Beverly let out a blood-curdling scream, ran to her bedroom, and barricaded the door. After much pleading and promises to protect her, Brock coaxed Beverly to come out. Looking at Jessie sitting on the death couch, Beverly felt warm liquid rising up in her throat. She excused herself, running to the bathroom to vomit.

Finally, all four were sitting in the same room. Jessie spoke first. "Beverly, I'm so sorry I scared you. I'm the twin sister of Jane Lawson. I didn't mean any harm. I know you're wondering why we are here. I'm going to have Brock explain what has happened."

Beverly nodded. Lily sat quietly beside her.

"When Jessie and I arrived at the cabin, John wasn't anywhere to be found. His things were still in the cabin. Nothing had been taken, not that we could tell. We checked the lake and the nearby woods. There was no sign of him. As luck would have it, we found him behind the cabin. He had been bitten by a timber rattler, twice, and was in very bad shape. He was shocked to see Jessie too," Brock said. "He said some things that I think you need to know."

"OK, but where is he? In the hospital? Can I go see him?" Beverly asked.

"Beverly... Honey, he was in *such* bad shape. We don't know how long he had been there. I'm sorry, but he passed away. Before he drew his last breath, he so much as confessed to killing Jane Lawson," Brock said softly. "He even said he left the body at the beach. There's just no doubt."

"*What?!* No, that can't be! That's not right. How could he say that?!" Beverly exclaimed. Her mind was reeling. *I did it! I did it! It was me, not John!*

"I'm so sorry. I wish it wasn't true. I wanted you to know before the media has a field day with it. Of course, they don't know you're his sister, so that's a blessing. Again, all of us at the agency are so sorry," Jessie said. "His body has been picked up at the airport and taken to the Curtis Funeral home in Eagle Hills."

Lily stood up as Brock and Jessie started to leave. "I'll stay with Beverly for a while and make sure she's OK."

After they left, Lily helped Beverly into the shower. All the crying had stopped, either from exhaustion or shock. Lily turned down the covers and helped Beverly into bed. "Don't turn the lamp off, please. I don't think I can handle the dark right now," Beverly whispered. "I'm OK. You can leave now. Thank you for all you've done, but I really need to be alone. John has always protected me; he protected me for one last time before he died. Now, you go on home, Lily. Love you, girlfriend."

"Are you sure you're going to be all right alone tonight? I don't mind staying overnight, if that's what you want."

"Honestly, I'm going to be fine. Lock the door when you leave."

Lily straightened up the living room, cleaned up the kitchen, and quietly left. She felt so bad for Beverly. As she walked back to her cottage, her thoughts were of her friend. *To find out you have a brother after all those years and then to lose him so quickly must be just terrible. Since I don't have any siblings, it's hard for me to understand. But for sure, she's going to have a hard time dealing with this.*

That evening, still with so much on her mind, Lily returned to her bench to try to bring some peace back within herself. She felt grateful for all her blessings, her good health, her friends, her home. She stared up at the clear night sky, decorated with twinkling stars and a bright crescent moon. The ocean's frothy waves pounded the beach. She wrapped her old quilt around her legs as a cool breeze nipped the air.

In the quiet of nature, she was suddenly interrupted by a furry friend. "Sam! Where did you come from?" The dog laid her head on Lily's lap. Max came up from behind the bench.

"Max, this is such a nice surprise. I didn't hear you drive up. Come sit down beside me," Lily said. "The night is so peaceful."

"I cut the lights and parked not far from here. It's a habit I guess I'll need to break." He laughed. "I was hoping you would be home."

Max stood in front of Lily and took her hand. "Come with me, Lily. There's something I've been waiting to say to you for a long time."

They walked down to the edge of the salty water. He smiled. "You are so beautiful, Lily." The shimmering moonlight cast an aura around the woman he loved. He held her face in his hands, tenderly kissing her forehead like he had the first night he walked her home. She trembled, hoping he was about to say what she yearned to hear.

"I love you, Lily Roberts. I have loved you for a long time," Max said. "All I can offer is to love you forever."

Hearing his words brought tears. She dared to hope for this moment. "I love you, Max Trainor. I will always love you."

Against the backdrop of that beautiful night, their professed love created a portrait of warmth and deep devotion. With Sam leading the way, Max and Lily walked down the beach hand in hand.

THE END

COMING SOON
Dark Passion

News reporter, Madison Pope, eagerly anticipates a relaxing vacation after covering a grueling six week court trial in her native town of Charlotte, North Carolina. However, her visit to the tiny coastal town of Eagle Hills brings unexpected challenges, including an awakening of raw passion.

Unable to deny the sensual tension building between herself and the town deputy, Madison is soon drawn into a seductive battle of wills, quickly complicated by the gruesome murder of a young woman.

When her reporting skills are needed, Madison joins a former military secret ops agent, a street savvy retired cop, and the town deputy to find the killer. The investigation is shadowed by subtle warnings and veiled threats, seemingly confined to Madison as she veers from the beaten path.

Will the town deputy succumb to Madison's erotic desires? Will the crime be solved or will the demented killer zero in on the news reporter as his next victim?